TYEHN

CONQUERED WORLD: BOOK FIFTEEN

ELIN WYN

CLOCK
WALK
PUBLISHING

TYEHN

White flakes swirled in the stiff coastal breeze, feeling like gentle fingers massaging my skin. With a smile on my face, I stood in the Kaster city square next to Jalok as the deluge continued. The snow had covered the stones of the square, making it seem like a solid sheet instead of segmented concrete.

"Isn't this great, Jalok?"

Jalok muttered something incomprehensible and sneezed. He pulled up the collar of his winter coat and huddled within its confines.

Jalok shot me a dirty look, snow piling on his scalp.

"No, it's not great. Leave it to a Valorni to think this inhospitable weather is somehow a positive."

"Bah, come on. Don't you just love the way it

blankets everything with a pristine coat? Like we're on a planet untouched by sapient incursion."

Our voices had a muted edge due to the snow absorbing sound.

I found the crisp, fresh snow to be bracing and invigorating. It made everything new, like it was a world that could have a fresh start.

Void knew, Ankou could use one.

My companion, apparently, didn't enjoy it as much.

"It's cold, it's wet, and I think I'm coming down with something, so why don't you just can the relentless cheer and let me suffer in silence?"

I chuckled at his griping.

"Come on, Jalok, doesn't your girlfriend live in this city?"

"What's that got to do with anything, you overgrown oaf?"

"You should think about how much fun you're going to have once you're off duty rather than complaining about the snow, that's all I'm saying"

His expression softened about one iota, but I figured that was the best I was going to get out of the grumpy Skotan.

We stood outside of the government building on the edge of the public square, having finished our recon and awaiting further instructions from our team leader

Sk'lar. It was kind of boring, to be honest, but the snow was a wonderful distraction.

"Jalok, did you know that every inch of snow equals ten inches of rain?"

"No, and I don't give a srell."

"Well, you should. Think about it."

"I don't want to. I just want to get out of this damn cold. The Skotan home world isn't plagued by this revolting phenomenon you seem so enchanted by."

"If this were rain and not snow, we'd have had twenty inches by now. The square would be flooded, and it would be even worse."

"That is a matter of opinion."

We were not just in Kaster because Jalok's girlfriend lived there. The anti-alien movement had been building momentum in this area, and Strike Team Three had been reassigned here.

The blanket of fresh snow disguised numerous stains—some of them from blood—on the square due to the recent riots.

It was hard not to take it personally when a growing contingent of humans were out protesting our rights to exist.

They had the right to free speech, of course.

And honestly, I never expected everyone to always get along.

But the more radicalized elements of their movement had taken to acts of sabotage and terrorism, attacking humans as well as aliens.

We could take it, but the humans were more fragile.

Things had been peaceful for a short while, but we all knew that it could boil over again at any time.

Which is why we'd been dispatched here. Without the use of the rifts, we couldn't always deploy rapidly enough to prevent more violence.

Finally, our comm units crackled, picking up static from the storm, and Sk'lar's curt voice came over the line.

"Jalok and Tyehn, report."

"Just finished a circuit of the square, Commander." I smiled down at Jalok. "Now we're enjoying the weather."

Jalok flipped me the bird, a gesture he picked up from the humans, and I chuckled anew. Apparently, the middle finger represents a human phallic symbol.

Human men must be tiny.

"Did you see anything amiss?"

"Negative, Commander. The snow is keeping the anti-alienists inside today, it seems."

"They're smarter than us." Jalok was smart enough to keep his grumbling off comms.

Sk'lar was a real ball buster, and getting laid hasn't mellowed him out as much as we'd hoped.

"I see. It doesn't hurt to be cautious, however. You two should make another circuit of the square, and then head over to Cazak and Navat's position."

"Copy that. Tyehn out."

"Damn it, he wants us to do more walking in this frozen rain?"

"Actually, Jalok, despite common belief, snow is not, in fact, frozen rain. That's a different atmospheric phenomenon. Rather, the water in the atmosphere condenses directly—"

"For fuck's sake, shut up. We're not all hydrologists, you know. All I want is a warm heating unit and a cold brew, not to have a science lesson."

"Suit yourself."

I didn't take Jalok's complaints personally.

Everyone knows he's got an attitude. The less generous would say he's a pain in the ass—another human expression, and this time it made sense.

We walked back out from under the awning under which we'd stood—not that it kept the snow off much anyway, or at least not enough to keep Jalok from complaining.

Our footprints were already half filled before we'd made it a hundred yards. I glanced behind us, seeing a large set and a smaller set trailing behind us.

Nothing else. No one was out in this weather, at least not marching around.

"I wish the anti-alienists were up to no good today. A good fight might actually warm me up some." Jalok muttered. "Dottie wouldn't have to find out."

I decided to be a bit sympathetic. Jalok wasn't really a man who'd expected to find his mate on an alien world, if ever.

Learning that she didn't exactly approve of his more violent tendencies had been a bit of a shock. He'd done well, toning things down, but it had taken a toll on his already rough temper.

"Why don't we swing by the main avenue after our next sweep? There's a coffee stand there. We can warm up for a bit and take it to go."

"Finally, you say something that doesn't piss me off. Good thinking, for a Valorni."

I glanced at him askance. "Aren't you a little bit troubled by the irony of making racist remarks while we're on patrol for people who are, in fact, racist?"

"More like species-ist, but I get your point. I just don't give a srell."

We grew silent, trudging on through the snow for a time with only our muted footfalls and his occasional sneezes to keep us company.

A human woman glared out of a second story apartment at us, her gaze full of suspicion. I smiled and waved at her cheerfully. Her sneer grew by a mile before she jerked her curtains shut.

"Why do you keep trying?"

"Diplomacy is the first recourse, remember? Then de-escalation, and then, finally, if there's no other alternative, reasonable force."

"I don't need a reason to use force. Force is its own reason."

I couldn't help but laugh at his gung-ho attitude.

Skotans are known to be hot tempered, but Jalok was like a Skotan with a little extra Skotan added in.

We reached the café I'd mentioned, cheerfully lit, warm and inviting. We headed inside and were enveloped by the heat coming from an overhead vent. Jalok paused directly underneath, opening his collar to let the warm air flow into his uniform.

"Hello." I smiled huge at the human attendant.

Her gaze was as cold as the snow, maybe even colder. I could tell she was considering giving us a hard time for being 'aliens' but I pulled my lapel back on the coat to reveal the insignia of Strike Team Three.

That made a huge difference in her service, if not her attitude. Sure, every alien she'd ever seen was part of the military, one way or another.

But it was one thing to give a hard time to someone who was passing through.

Something else entirely when it was someone stationed here, working with the local guards.

I ordered two coffees.

I couldn't resist taking a sip right away at the counter, and then carried our cups to the high pub table Jalok had chosen.

He sneered at me and shook his head as I deposited his drink in front of him.

"What's wrong? I thought you liked this bitter swill."

"The problem's not the drink." He pointed at my face. "It's the whipped cream on your big honking nose. You look ridiculous."

"Oh." I chuckled as I used my tongue to lick the dollop of cream off my nose. "Did I get it?"

"Ugh, yes, you disgusting freak. Next time use a napkin."

I shrugged and sat down across from him. Technically we were on duty, but a with the snow blanketing the city, Kaster is dead as can be. I figured a few minutes sipping drinks to warm both Jalok's body and his attitude wouldn't be too gross a dereliction of duty.

"So, how are things going with Dottie?"

Jalok almost smiled—almost.

"Good." He drank from his cup, not bothering to blow on it to cool the liquid.

"Good? That's all I'm getting out of you?"

"Well, I'm not going to describe our sex life, if that's what you were wondering."

It wasn't what I had been wondering about, but

quite frankly I was a bit curious as to what it would be like to sleep with a human woman.

So many of our crew had found their mates, but I still hadn't seen the attraction.

They were interesting...but nothing had ever sparked inside me when I'd seen one.

"I don't expect you to give me intimate details, just... what's it like? Being with a human, I mean. Does she get freaked out by your scales?"

"No." He took a drink of his coffee and sighed. "Now this is good."

"I heard Dottie didn't like you at first."

Jalok glared at me over his steaming cup.

"Who the hell told you that?"

"I don't remember, probably Cazak."

"Figures."

"They said that when you went berserk during the riots and put all those people in the hospital she was a little spooked, but then you guys became friends."

"Look, you go ahead and believe what you want. Doesn't matter to me a lick. Now finish your drink before Sk'lar starts complaining—oh, speak of the devil."

Our comms lit up, and sure enough Sk'lar demanded to know why we hadn't returned to our assigned position.

I drained the remains of my drink in one big gulp and hastily followed Jalok back into the snow.

MAKI

I gave my ropes three sharp tugs and pulled at the clasps of my harness. One of the clasps was a little rusty so I switched it out for a new one.

I went through harness clasps like those alien soldiers went through blaster ammo.

I checked the strength of the branch my ropes were tied to. Sturdy, healthy and perfect for ziplining.

Last month, I spent my whole day off trekking through the forest putting up the perfect ziplining course. It wasn't every day that I could do something like that.

I had to wait until all of the forest creatures were either in hibernation or at least out of nesting season.

Nothing like overprotective mamas with four hundred teeth to ruin one's hike.

The living vines were a whole other story.

Some of them belong to the Puppet Master who, by all means, is a real pal. The others belonged to an array of species that liked to wrap around my ankles and attempt to drag me underground.

Figuring out which was which was always good fun.

I tentatively touched the weapon at my side.

It was of my own invention, specially designed to handle those pesky living vines that were friends rather than foes.

Unfortunately, those nasty vines looked just like the Puppet Master's friendly tendrils. At least once, I've stabbed the needle-thin barred blade of my weapon into the flesh of the Puppet Master.

I'd never spoken to the Puppet Master but I'd heard from some of my coworkers that if someone touches the Puppet Master, it can hear their thoughts.

Since my mother raised me right, the moment I realized I stabbed the wrong vine, I pressed my hand into the Puppet Master and apologized profusely.

I swore I heard it laugh.

Ever since that day, I felt safer going on my solo excursions in the forest.

It was like I had a spotter without having to deal with the company of people who didn't know what they were doing.

Maybe it wasn't the brightest plan, depending on a

giant plant-creature I'd never seen, but it made sense in my head.

My coworkers thought I was insane for doing this sort of stuff on my day off. Most of them liked to sit in dark pubs or take shuttles to the bigger cities on their days off.

That sounded boring to me but I didn't judge them for it.

Except... shopping. Really?

It wasn't my fault that I was born with a high adventure drive.

I entirely blamed my father, and thanked him as well.

He had a lust for adventure too. I learned everything I knew about handling myself in the wilderness from him.

Nearly every weekend of my childhood was spent camping, climbing, and jumping off things no rational person would ever jump off.

My happiest memories were spent in the basement where my mother worked in her at-home lab.

Best childhood ever.

I tipped my face to the sunlight and let it warm my skin. A gentle breeze picked up. Without opening my eyes, I stepped off the branch.

My weight settled quickly and comfortably into my harness as I zipped through the trees. Birds and other small forest creatures darted out of my way as I came as close to flying as I'd ever get.

I landed on the platform at the end of the zip line.

One click to clip myself to the next line, and another to free me from the last one and I was on my way. I'd gotten the zipline transfer movements down to a science.

One of the questions I was often asked was why do I put hours of effort into a zipline excursion that ultimately lasts less than ten minutes.

What people didn't understand is that the trek all the way out here, the preparation, and the double-checking were all part of the fun.

The final ride was almost a bonus, seeing how all your planning worked out.

The forest started to thin out as I zipped down the last leg of my self-made course. My bike waited where I parked it at the base of the final tree. As I flew through the canopy, I loosed a sigh of relief.

On more than one occasion, I'd finished a hike or a zip line course to find that my bike had been moved somewhere.

Probably the work of any number of forest dwellers. Either that or a disturbingly dedicated prankster.

With adrenaline coursing through my veins, I unhooked my harness and practically slid down the tree trunk.

And that's where my perfect day hit its first bump.

A blinking red light on my comm unit.

My stomach tightened for a moment. A message from home?

I hit play, and gnawed at my lip, only relaxing when my boss's voice filled the forest air. "Maki, I know it's your day off, but I need you to stop by." Dr. Illiux Band laughed. "You'll find it interesting."

Ooh.

I'd finished my last assignment a few days ago, and had been anxious to see what was next.

It might be fair to say I had a low boredom threshold.

Maybe.

A friend of mine helped me rig up my bike a few years back. Instead of an ignition, all my sweet baby needed was a handprint scan. It would only start for me.

If I wanted to, I could calibrate someone else's handprint into the bike's memory stores so that they could start my bike.

It went without saying that I never wanted to do that.

There was a greater chance of me ziplining between the stars without a helmet than letting someone else ride my bike.

I placed my handprint on the scanner between the handlebars.

My buddy also installed a small console so I could get in touch with people should I get in an accident, use my navigational tracker in unfamiliar territory, and participate in conference calls while I'm en route to a job site.

The handprint scanner flared green as my bike started up. The tire rims lit up bright blue. Blue streaks of light ignited over the black frame. The engine was blessedly quiet. The best thing my father ever taught me was how to listen to nature. As much as I loved my bike, I didn't like that it disrupted the natural sounds around me so I had that remedied.

Now, my bike was the perfect vehicle. It was jungle friendly, desert friendly and city friendly which was perfect since I spent an equal amount of time in all three settings. Mountains? No problem.

Rocky terrain? Easy as Qigla pie.

My stomach rumbled.

Wow, I could go for a Qigla pie right about now. I already ate through the nutrient bars I packed this morning.

No matter how many times I'd done this, I've never correctly anticipated how many nutrient bars it takes to fill me up.

As I rumbled through the jungle on my bike, I

spied an unusually dense looking patch of earth. I gently slowed my bike and hopped off. I picked up a pinch of dirt and rolled it between my fingers. It had an odd texture. I couldn't say I'd ever left something similar. It hadn't eaten away at my skin so that was a good sign.

The earth around Sauma was amazing. There were soil concentrations only found in this area. That's why I moved here to work.

I pulled a sample vial out of my pack and scooped up some of the dirt. This would be fun to analyze later.

I didn't like sitting still for extended periods of time.

When I first moved to Sauma, I loved being in the lab day in and day out. I got that from my mother.

After a month or so, I started getting restless. Luckily, there were a number of clubs in Sauma.

I was in a club for other bikers. We rode together once a week though sometimes I met up with a handful of people just for quick rides.

I was also part of a free-running group. We specialized in leaping through abandoned buildings.

Actually, it was through a member of the free-running group that I discovered an archaeology team that occasionally sourced locals from Sauma to work on their digs.

As someone who was interested in archaeology but not fully trained, I signed up the first chance I got.

Digs didn't happen very often, but I relished them all the same, even if it was just for grunt work.

Forest gave way to outpost shacks and farms then eventually to city streets. I wove through pedestrians with ease until I reached my building.

My boss, Dr. Illiux Band, was waiting for me when I walked in the door.

"Sorry for calling you in on your day off but it couldn't wait," he grinned. "Here's your next assignment." He passed me a datapad. "We have a team on a new project and you know the rules - they're going to need an independent observer to help and make sure everything is right and proper."

I opened up the tab with the location information first and imported it into my bike's console.

"You're going to the Sika Jungle. It's not far. You should be able to get there in less than an hour on that bike of yours."

I analyzed the map that popped up on my console. Five trails to the site appeared on the console, four of which I was already familiar with.

"I'll head out now," I told my boss. "There's an unexplored trail that's calling my name."

"Don't get yourself killed before you get there," he warned me.

"I would never dream of being that rude."

TYEHN

J alok and I trudged up the ramp leading inside our shuttle craft.

The rest of team three was already on board as our eyes adjusted to the relative gloom. After being outside in the blazing white of a snowstorm, the shuttle's cabin seemed darker than a cave.

I bumped Navat's closed fist by way of greeting as I settled into the seat next to him. As the only other Valorni on Team Three, we took care of each other.

It's weird, because had it not been for the stranding I doubt we would have been friends. Before we joined the crew of the *Vengeance*, I'd been a scientist, and he was a laborer, so other than being of the same species we don't have a lot in common.

Then the Xathi came, and we all had to become soldiers.

Even now that the bugs seem a past threat, we continued on in our new roles, only now our enemies were food shortages and political unrest.

The more things changed, the more they stayed the same, or so the humans said.

"For fuck's sake, close the damn ramp." Jalok shivered, and added a sneeze for emphasis.

"Not yet." Sk'lar peered out the back of the shuttle. "We have one more passenger."

"What? But the squad's all here."

Jalok craned his neck about, searching the cabin for the rest of our team.

"I see Cazak's ugly ass, and the two big cows, and a beady eyed K'ver, and I know I'm sitting here on account of the fact that I'm freezing to death. Who the hell else is left? Did we get a new recruit?"

Sk'lar grins wryly at Jalok.

"We're taking a scientist with us as well who needs a lift to the capital. Bide."

"I don't want to bide. When the scientist gets here, I'm going to kick his ass for making me cold." He scowled. "I've got two weeks of furlough coming, and want to get something nice for Dottie."

Light footfalls barely made an echo on the ramp,

announcing a new passenger coming onboard. When I saw who it was, I had to stifle a laugh.

Cazak noticed too, and shot his cousin Jalok a wry grin.

"What was that you were saying about our passenger?" Cazak's tone dripped with nonchalant innocence. Jalok noticed it, but being Jalok he didn't stop to ponder the significance of it.

"I said, I'm gonna kick their ass."

The scientist stood behind Jalok's chair, arms crossed over her chest. She glanced around the cabin, took in our stifled smiles, and got herself up to speed really quick.

"Just like you did to those rioters a while back, right?" Navat prodded.

Like a good little fish, Jalok rose to the bait.

"No, not just like the rioters. What I do to this human is going to make me seem like a pacifist. I'll break his arms, his legs, and then knock all his teeth out for good measure."

"You're going to knock my teeth out?"

Jalok's eyes went wide when he heard Dottie's voice. He leaped to his feet and turned around, face a mask of incredulity.

"Dottie? You're the scientist?"

"Oh, don't let me stop you, babe, you're on a roll."

She raised an eyebrow and glared. Jalok squirmed under her disapproving gaze.

"I—that is, I didn't know it would be—you look pretty today, babe."

The rest of Team Three—even Sk'lar, let out an *aww* in unison as if to say, how cute.

Jalok gritted his teeth and tried to keep a smile on his face, even though we all knew he was fuming.

"Thanks." Dottie got on her tip toes and kissed Jalok on the cheek. His tension and anger seemed to drain away.

"Ah, I'm sure you know everyone here, right Dottie?"

I marveled at the way that Jalok's whole demeanor changed with Dottie present. It was almost like he wasn't an insufferable srell.

Almost.

"You know Cazak's ugly ass, of course, but the big bald guy with purple stripes on his shoulders is Tyehn. You two should get along great, given he's a scientist."

"Charmed." I offered my hand for a shake, as was the human custom. Her hand was swallowed by my much larger mitt.

"Likewise."

"The other big, bald guy is Navat."

"Pleased to meet you."

"And you as well."

"We're glad you're here, Dottie."

Dottie turned to Cazak and arched an eyebrow.

"Why is that?"

"Because Jalok is so much less of a dick when you're around."

"Aww, thanks guys." Dottie smiled sweetly at Cazak. Jalok tried to pretend he wasn't furious with his cousin with limited success.

The ramp finally closed up. Jalok and Dottie took up seats near the rear of the shuttle while the rest of us politely pretended they were not present.

"So what are you going to do with your furlough, Tyehn?"

I glanced over at Cazak and shrugged.

"I'm not sure. I'd like to hang out with some of the new friends I've made, both human and otherwise. You?"

"I'm going to try and find a nice hole in the wall and drink myself into oblivion, like I do every furlough."

As if in answer to our planning, Sk'lar headed up to the cockpit as an emergency comm came through.

He listened to it grimly, spoke quietly to the person on the other end, and returned minutes later, his lips a thin, tight line.

"Bad news, Team Three."

"Isn't it always?"

Sk'lar ignored Cazak's comment.

"It looks like our furlough's been canceled."

"What? No way." Jalok seemed particularly disgruntled, even for him. I guess he was planning on spending some quality time with Dottie.

"So, we're not going to Nyheim?" I asked.

"We're going to Nyheim, but the team will remain on call. That means no getting piss drunk in case we get called out on a mission."

"What happened?"

Sk'lar turns to Navat grimly.

"There's been some 'civil unrest' at one of the smaller colonies up the coast. Security forces have it handled—for now—but we're going to remain on alert in case they need back up."

All of Team Three displayed their dismay as per their own way. Jalok complained, Navat sighed heavily, Cazak shook his head, and I merely shrugged. I was disappointed as much as the others, but I didn't see a point it getting all worked up over it.

We spent most of the ride to Nyheim in silence, all lost in our own thoughts. The exceptions were Dottie and Jalok, who continued to converse in low tones at the rear of the shuttle.

Our craft lurched to a stop, the landing pylons came down, and soon we were all tramping down the ramp.

"Remember, we're on call." Sk'lar glared at Cazak in

particular. "You'd better be fit for duty when and if the call comes in."

"Yes sir."

Cazak gave a sarcastic salute that became an obscene gesture when Sk'lar turned his back to converse with our pilot.

"Who's hungry?"

Cazak and Navat turned to face me, as Dottie and Jalok strode off through the snow, hand in hand.

Part of me envied what they had, but I'd never be attracted to a human woman.

"Are you buying?"

"Not likely. I thought we'd go hit that ramen place Sylor took us to last time we were here."

"Sounds good to me."

"Me, too."

The three of us traipsed through the snowfall into Nyheim's busy downtown area. Most folks were friendly, especially the merchants—everyone knew soldiers had credits to spare when off duty—but some of the humans gave us baleful glares.

It seemed like the anti-alien sentiment had spread all over the colonies.

We did our best to ignore the glares and made our way to the ramen place. Navat pushed the door open, and we were greeted by a warm blast of air and the inviting smell of noodles and soup.

My belly rumbled like thunder as we strode up to the counter and made our orders.

Soon we were ensconced at a booth near the corner of the room, so we could watch all around us. With all of the anti-alien sentiment going around, we figured it couldn't hurt to be cautious.

As the three of us chowed down on our dinner, I couldn't help but overhear snippets of the myriad conversations going on around the diner. A lot of folks were talking—or more aptly, complaining—about the snowfall, which made sense.

There were more than a few people worried about food shortages. Supposedly, that situation was pretty much handled, but it didn't mean that people weren't still worried about it.

A few others talked about whether or not we could really trust the Puppet Master, but it was the pair at the booth next to us that was of particular interest.

One was a Valorni like myself and Navat, and he had his left arm in a sling. His human companion seemed to be inquiring about the injury.

"Does it hurt much?"

"Not anymore. The medics said I'd be able to lose the sling tomorrow, but it's a precaution."

"And you say Marin just flipped out on you? Out of nowhere."

"Yeah. One minute we were joking about how

General Rouhr gets that line between his eyes when he's angry, the next he's going off on me about how I'm alien scum and I need to get off 'his' planet."

"The fuck, man?"

"I know. Then he grabbed a coil spanner and stabbed me in the arm with it."

"Wow. Did he get arrested?"

"You think? Of course, he did. But I was talking to the guards, and it seems like he's not the only guy to just sort of lose it lately. From zero to full on xenophobe in a second flat."

The three of us at our table exchanged glances. We'd all heard of someone who'd had a sudden, drastic change in attitude. Brass said it was being looked into, but that didn't reassure us.

Not in the least.

MAKI

Lucky for me that I started my journey to the Sika Jungle early enough in the afternoon to make time for exploring.

Hopefully Dr. Band hadn't told whoever I'm supposed to report to that I was going to be there at a certain time.

It was impossible for me not to go off trail once I entered the forest.

Too many interesting things lay around every tree and rock, waiting for me to explore.

I hadn't spent much time in the Sika Jungle, but I'd ridden through it a handful of times with the biker club.

The trail I currently rode down was all new to me. To the average person, one chunk of forest looked just like another. I'd spent years training myself to recognize subtle differences in the earth and foliage.

Perhaps what was the most exciting thing about the Sika Jungle was that it was our planet's only snowy jungle.

That we knew of, of course.

So little of our planet had been explored since colonization. How exciting was that?

My heart sped up at the thought of it.

I slowed my bike so that I could take in the scenery. The Sika forest was still verdant and lush even though it was covered in a blanket of silvery-white fluff. It some places, it was so thick that everything within my field of vision was a sea of white.

I STOPPED and took samples of the snow. I'd already taken samples before but they didn't yield any satisfying answers.

Once the snow was cleared as non-toxic, non-cancerous, and non-allergenic all research halted to focus on more pressing matters. That doesn't mean I don't want to know where it comes from or what it is.

Careful to keep my bike in sight, I walked up a rocky incline. I stepped carefully. My boots were built to handle even the most unsteady terrains, but they weren't built with frost in mind. I bent down and touched a latticework frost that covered a stone. It wasn't cold.

Earth frost would've melted under my touch but not this.

I wondered if it was some kind of moss or maybe a mineral. I took a scraping of the frost to compare it's make up to that of the snow and pressed on. When I reached the small peak of the incline, I stopped to observe my surroundings.

Every inch of the trees was covered in snow and frost. There weren't as many leaves up here. The trees looked strangely bare compared to the ones growing at lower elevations. Most remarkable of all were the frost formations dripping off the spindly branches.

From what I could tell, the bioluminescent moss known to grow on this species of tree mixed in with the frost as it formed.

The moss faintly glowed when it wasn't exposed in direct sunlight producing suspended droplets of lilac, mint green, and pale blue.

I stood still, closed my eyes, and listened to the sounds of the jungle. It was eerily quiet compared to the forest I'd been in earlier today.

Sometimes, when I cleared my mind and listened with all of my being, I felt a hum of energy emanated from the earth beneath me. I felt that same hum now.

When I opened my eyes, I felt revitalized. Not that I

needed it. One nutrition bar had enough caffeine in it to make a Valorni feel twitchy and I'd eaten four before noon.

With all of my observation, listening, and general milling about I completely lost track of time. I rush-slash-fall down the rocky hill to my bike. I couldn't tell how long I'd been gone but if the fresh blanket of snow covering my bike was any indication, I'd been walking for a while.

The snow wasn't great for traction. I carefully wove my bike through the bioluminescent frost covered trees, careful not to disturb the beautiful bulbs.

I pulled up the location of my new assignment on the GPS. I hadn't read anything else on the datapad other than the location.

In my excitement, I didn't clear time to read through the dossier that Dr. Band no doubt packed with information. I planned to get to the location and take a few moments to brief myself but I'd wasted too much time wandering around in the forest.

Oh well. Totally worth it.

The GPS coordinates brought me to a clearing inside a little patch of snowy jungle. A small group of people had already gathered in the clearing. They all wore matching jackets bearing the name of a lab that I'd heard of once or twice but didn't know much about.

EcoBright Laboratories.

The three members of the EcoBright team, two men and one woman, looked at me as I slowly approached on my bike.

"Excuse me," the woman called out. "This area is closed off for testing. You'll have to turn around."

"I'm the geoscientist from Sauma. Dr. Band would have told you about me."

I was used to the look of surprise people gave me when I told them my profession. I didn't look the part of a geoscientist, whatever that meant.

Maybe they expected someone who was never seen without their white lab coat who wasn't capable of functioning outside of a lab.

The woman looked the most surprised out of the three EcoBright team members.

"Yes," the smaller of the two men spoke up when no one else did. "He sent us a message telling us you were on the way."

"Four hours ago," the woman said pointedly.

"I wasn't told anyone would be here," I replied. "Had I known I would've hustled. I couldn't help but stop to admire the snowy forest. Isn't it stunning?"

"For the first twenty minutes, yeah. The charm wears off when you're dumping snow out of every piece of clothing and still find some in your bed the next day," the other man says.

I laughed but stopped when I realized he wasn't making a joke.

I powered down my bike and walked over to the group.

"Do you have a name, geoscientist?" the taller of the two men asked.

"Maki Hotaru." I stuck out my hand and gave his hand a firm shake, which took him by surprise. I loved catching people off guard. It was fun to see what people do when their expectations aren't met.

"I'm Tovin, he's Cam, and that's Lorrva."

After we get through the pleasantries, I was eager to get to work.

"What have you been working on so far?"

"We're tracking the differences in the soil since the Puppet Master started actively participating in the planet's agricultural program," Lorrva explained.

"I didn't realize EcoBright was involved with the Puppet Master and the Nyheim operations," I replied.

Nyheim's headed up just about every public interest project since the Xathi were defeated and our planet started pulling itself back together.

I'd noticed that the mayor of Nyheim and her partner, an alien General, liked to hire skilled individuals from other labs and occasionally contract work out to entire labs as well.

It was a smart move, getting more humans involved,

spreading out the work. But I hadn't heard about EcoBright being contracted.

"We aren't affiliated with the Nyheim operations at the moment," Tovin explained. "EcoBright is being privately funded for this operation. But to stay in compliance, we are required to host you and maintain independent oversight."

"Oh." I furrowed my brows.

"Nyheim doesn't have the power to decide what private labs pursue in their research," Lorrva said in a matter-of-fact tone. "However, we aren't going to hoard our findings. They'll be made public knowledge so everyone can benefit from them."

"Found anything worth publishing?" I asked, hoping to skip past the politics.

"Not yet. We've only just gotten started. When we were informed we'd have to have independent oversight to avoid being shut down, Dr. Band recommended you highly," Cam said.

"Well, I don't like to brag," I shrugged.

"Take a look at the photos," Lorrva pushed the conversation on.

I retrieved the datapad from my pack and flipped to the photos. The first one was of a section of forest though everything was dead and the snow was brown rather than gleaming white.

"Is this the clearing we're standing in now?" I pointed to the picture.

"The very same," Cam said. "That was taken a week after Nyheim and the Puppet Master forged an alliance."

"The Puppet Master did this in that short of a time span?" I marveled.

"Yes. We're here to figure out how the Puppet Master did this and how we can replicate it. Our goal is to make replication possible at the household level so people can have their own rapid growth gardens."

"Incredible." I flip through the growth projections on the datapad. "This sounds like an exciting project."

"We aren't here for the excitement." Lorrva fixed me with a look that was far from friendly. "We're here to help the food crisis."

"What's more exciting than figuring out a way to make sure every single person has enough food?" I replied. "Besides, I love cracking a good mystery."

"I like the way you think," Cam chuckled, earning a look of his own from Lorrva.

"So, you're in then?" Tovin asked.

"Absolutely."

TYEHN

W hen my mind is troubled, I find that physical exertion is a great way to clear it. That's why I headed to the gym the next morning after our deployment to Nyheim where we would be staying in the Central Barracks.

I stepped into the gymnasium and shook off the cold, hanging my coat on one of the provided hooks.

The place was nearly deserted, it being quite early. Only the real die-hard fitness buffs would bother being here just after the sun had peeked over the horizon. Not that I could see the sun at the time, given the snow that continued to fall.

After changing into my workout gear, I headed to the free weight section. I hung some metal plates on a dumbbell and set up for a bench press.

As I placed the last plate on and screwed down the clamps, the door opened up and my human friend Keith strode in.

"Greetings, Keith."

"Sup. You ready to start?"

"I was born ready."

We laughed even though it was an old, tired joke. Keith changed into his gear and came out just in time to spot me for my second set.

Keith was big for a human. His shoulders were broad and tapered down to a narrow waist. Then his thighs flared out like massive tree trunks. Obviously, I could out press him, given our anatomical differences, but Keith had been catching up fast. At the time, I was up to nearly half a ton on the bench press. Keith was pressing six hundred and on his way past that.

"Come on, big guy, you got to want it."

My voice was strained as I struggled to get the bar off my chest for the last rep.

"I do want it."

"You gotta want it bad."

"I want it...bad."

The bar moved two inches from my chest and then shivered there in my straining grip. Should I have lost it, Keith was there to catch it and avoid a broken sternum.

"You gotta want it real bad."

"I want it *real bad.*"

The bar rose up to the maximum, and I gratefully set it back on the rack with Keith's assistance.

"Not bad, buddy. Not bad at all."

"Yeah, let me just take away some weights here. Don't want you lifting as much as a man."

"Ha ha," he said. "Very funny."

We set up the bar and Keith did his sets with no problem.

As we moved about the gym using the various equipment, we chatted about current events. I hadn't been to Nyheim in a couple of weeks, so we had a bit to catch up on. Apparently Keith started dating a woman from one of the refugee camps, a medic or something.

"So when are you actually going to get laid, Tyehn?"

"As soon as I get off duty and the matriarch of your family signals my comm—"

"Bro, I told you. It's 'your mom gives me her number'. Anyway, it might help you lose some of this tension that's holding you back in the gym."

"Seen any Valorni women around?"

"No, but I've seen plenty of human women. Look, chicks dig big dudes. Why do you think I started working out in the first place?"

I grunted out a reply as I shoved the weight bar up

over my head for the final rep. As it settled back down, I fixed him with a glare.

"I'm way too busy for dealing with any of that srell right now. The anti alien riots have been keeping us jumping like dogs."

"Like frogs. The phrase is jumping like frogs."

"Dogs aren't the little green hairless ones?"

"No, they're the hairy ones that bite."

"Well, jumping like one of those other things, then."

Keith took his place and started banging out his sets. The smug bastard could talk and lift at the same time.

"Man, that anti alien shit is such bull. People are people. Don't matter what planet they're from."

"I heard that."

"I should hope so, you're standing right next to me."

"Such a comedian. So funny I forgot to laugh."

He finished his set while I jumped onto the squat press. I was slapping plates onto the bar, getting ready for some serious hanging and banging, when Keith all of the sudden grabbed his head and swayed on his feet.

"What's the matter? You getting a cold from all this snow?"

Keith looked up at me, confusion in his gaze. Then, a weird flash went across his eyes. His gaze suddenly narrowed, and his face grew red.

"You alien son of a bitch."

"What?" I laughed, thinking he was kidding. "Not funny."

"You aren't going to eat our food and steal our women anymore."

"What? You were just saying that I should—"

Keith snarled and lashed out at me with a fist. His speed was incredible, and before I could react he'd smashed my nose good. Blood spurted from my face as I backpedaled away from his hostile advance.

"Keith? What's wrong?"

"Die, alien asshole!"

Keith leaned to the side and unleashed a furious snap kick. I managed to deflect most of the blow from its intended target—my groin—but my forearms ached from the impact. Keith was strong as hell.

"What's gotten into you? Snap out of it."

His face a mask of rage, Keith raised his hands into a boxing stance and unleashed a dozen blows in a flurry. Despite my greater reach, he managed to tag me two more times, once in the solar plexus and once in the jaw. My face and gut stinging, I continued to back away before his assault.

The only problem was that there wasn't much room to retreat. Soon I was going to have to run or fight, and since Keith was between me and the exit fleeing didn't seem a good option.

I raised my hands up in standard Valorni hand to hand position, with one arm slightly bent at my waist, and the other up in guard position. I deflected a few more of his blows, but then he threw in a knee that caught me right in the groin.

My cry of pain mixed with the slap of bone on bone as our scuffle continued. I gave up all hope of reasoning with him and concentrated on defense, because he was my friend and I didn't want to hurt him.

I thought back to what was said last night, about how people had been suddenly changing their entire attitudes and growing violent. It appeared it was no longer a second hand experience for me.

Soon, it became woefully obvious that I could not remain on the defensive. Keith was a good fighter, well trained in his world's martial arts. Given his greater speed, and surprisingly nearly equal strength, I took a half dozen more good shots and was now spattering the gym mats with my blood.

I had to go on the offensive. Keith came in for a superman punch, actually flying off his feet and extending his arm for more power. I caught his wrist, and pivoted on my back foot to send him flying over my shoulder. He crashed to the floor, and I held onto his arm in a joint lock for good measure.

"Keith snap out of it, man. Can you hear me?"

"Fuck you, alien scum."

Keith couldn't escape from my joint lock without risking a broken arm, but he found another way. His leg snapped up and caught me square in the jaw. Reeling, I stumbled back a few feet, releasing his arm.

He went right back on the attack, landing another hard roundhouse kick to my temple. The gym walls started wavering, my vision growing dark as I struggled to hold on to consciousness.

Then Keith upped the ante. He grabbed a twenty pound barbell and hurled it at me. I just barely ducked my head out of its path, but the iron weight still clipped me painfully on the shoulder.

Keith hurled another one at me before I closed the distance. We grappled for a bit, and I trapped his arms to the side in a bearhug. Now my greater strength came into play and he couldn't budge.

"Srell, Keith. Don't make me hurt you."

His response was to snap his head forward, smashing the bridge of my nose with his brow. As pain exploded in my face, I lost my grip on him. Keith snarled like an animal and tackled me around the waist. He bulled me back a few yards until I spread my feet wide and stopped our momentum.

"Sorry Keith, you're not giving me a choice here."

If I didn't do something to stop Keith, he was going

to kill me. As he redoubled his efforts to knock me flat, I bent over and wrapped my arms around his waist. With a grunt of exertion and pain from the numerous injuries he'd inflicted, I straightened my torso and pulled him into the air.

Keith wound up with the small of his back over my shoulder, legs dangling over the other side. Before he could react, I brought him back down, straight onto his head and shoulders. Keith hit hard, his eyes going glassy for a moment, but then he started struggling again.

Fortunately, I'd retained my grip around his waist. I lifted him into the air a second time and power bombed him back to the mat. This time he bounced a foot into the air and then lay still, eyes closed.

"Keith. I'm sorry. I'm sorry."

He groaned a little bit, meaning he was still alive.

I bundled him up into my arms like a child and carried him out into the cold, even though I was still in my skimpy gym gear.

I ran all the way to the detention center, because I knew there was a medic always on duty and he needed to be locked up before he hurt someone. Well, someone else.

I explained everything to Evie, the current person in charge. I stressed several times that Keith was my friend, and he was not like this. Not at all.

Evie promised to take good care of him, and I had nothing left to do but leave him in their care.

I couldn't stop thinking about the way he'd changed, that weird flash of light and how he'd become so vicious.

MAKI

After I agreed to work with Lorrva, Tovin, and Cam they brought in tents to set up a temporary lab in the area. Their equipment was pretty nice. Better than what I had to work with at my lab, at least. Though my lab was nothing compared to what they have set up in Nyheim.

I wasn't sure how I felt about what Lorrva told me the first day I met them.

Yes, I knew there were still privately funded labs on Ankou but I didn't realize any of them were up and running once more.

The Xathi didn't just topple our cities, they damn well toppled our economy. I wanted to know exactly who on this planet had enough spare money to fund a project like this.

My suspicions were probably misplaced. This project was all about making farming more accessible to the average person. That was a good thing that was also desperately needed. Still, I didn't like the fact that I didn't really feel like I knew who I was working for.

Dr. Band must've done some vetting before sending me off to supervise.

That counted for something.

Still, I'd been working with the EcoBright team for two days now and I couldn't say I fit in.

Obviously, I didn't get one of the cool matching jackets with my name on it but it was more than that.

None of the team members, not even Cam who I thought was the least likely to kill me with one look, were willing to share information.

New people joined the project every day so far. However, I noticed that the people who joined us yesterday were not the same people to show up at the site today. Only me, Lorrva, Tovin and Cam were the constants. I'd only been working here for two days but I expected this project to run like any other project.

There was almost zero collaboration.

Lorrva, Tovin, and Cam must have determined their daily tasks before anyone else arrived. That was the only explanation. They barely spoke to anyone, including each other, when they were at the site.

Yesterday, I noticed Tovin storing a soil sample at

the wrong temperature. I offered him help like any sane coworker would.

And...he didn't acknowledge me in any way.

Weird.

It was pretty damn hard to ignore the only person within one hundred yards. Especially if that person was me and I was hovering over his shoulder.

I planned to fix the sample, or take another one when his back was turned but he put the samples somewhere else.

The tents on site were small.

There were only so many places someone could hide something. I doubted that the official Nyheim labs had this much security.

What was even weirder was that I wasn't allowed in the tents. I didn't know what I was doing there on my second day. I'd never felt more useless in my life. I hated feeling useless. Why was I even here?

Miraculously, today I arrived before the odd trio and their band of ever-changing interns. Knowing my time was limited, I ducked into the first tent I saw. It was filled with portable lab equipment with exactly enough space for a single person to work.

There was something strange about the equipment. It wasn't the kind of equipment necessary for tracking growth.

I wasn't sure what the equipment was for but if they

wanted growth results, they weren't going to get it this way.

As strange as Lorrva, Tovin, and Cam were, I didn't once get the impression that they were incompetent. They must've known the experiments and tests they ran here wouldn't yield the results they told me they were looking for.

So, what was all this in aid of?

"You aren't supposed to be here." Tovin's voice nearly made me jump out of my skin. I whirled around, hand over my heart.

"You should wear a bell or something," I sputtered.

"This is a secure facility," he said with a straight face. I bit back a laugh.

"It's a tent in the middle of the woods. What's this stuff for?" I gestured to the equipment behind me.

"That's none of your concern," Tovin replied.

"Yes, it is." I folded my arms across my chest. "None of this correlates with the job description I was given."

The corner of Tovin's mouth twitched. I thought he was attempting to smile but it was far too unsettling to be a smile.

"What makes you think you're privy to every detail of this job?" He asked.

"This job is a joke," I snort. "No one lets me do anything. I can't even enter the tents. I'm the best geoscientist around, remember? Wouldn't that mean

I get to analyze what we find? Correction, what you find. I haven't been allowed to look for anything so it stands to reason that I haven't found anything."

"Are you finished?" Tovin had the nerve to look bored.

"No." I narrowed my eyes. "How did that sample from yesterday turn out? The condensation should've compromised anything worth analyzing by now. You'll have to collect a new sample if you want to test chemical levels."

"We aren't testing chemical levels," Tovin said. "We're testing soil composition and understanding the interconnectedness of all the flora."

"What did you say your background was?" I asked. "If your testing soil, you're looking at it's make up. That involves testing chemical levels."

"Gee, you really are the best," he snapped.

"I'm going to get started on my work." I tried to step past him but he wouldn't move.

"Where are you going?"

"You won't tell me anything. Why would I tell you anything?" I challenged.

"There have been reports of a sinkhole about half a click east of here," he said. "Just don't go over there. I don't want to be liable for you doing something reckless."

"I'm pretty good at avoiding sinkholes." I pushed past him and stepped back into the clearing.

Not surprisingly, I ran right into Lorrva.

"Can I help you?" She looked at me like she'd just caught me stealing.

"No, I'm the one who's supposed to help you. What do you want me to do today?"

"Don't interfere." She stepped around me and entered the tent. She closed the entrance flap. I heard something click into place. Figured that these people would know how to lock a tent.

Ridiculous.

With nothing to do, I felt restlessness creeping up on me. I wasn't up for another day of standing around and being ignored.

I looked to the east and a wicked smile spread across my mouth.

Did I want to walk half a click to the east just to spite Tovin?

Yes, I did.

Taking the bike would have been too noticeable despite the silence. I'd have to walk. I could take samples from the sinkhole as well. I'd come across dozens of sinkholes in my day. I knew how to be safe around them.

I walked over to my bike and grabbed my pack. It

had supplies for collecting samples, a harness, and a few lengths of rope.

If anything, I could tie myself off on a tree while I poked around the edges of the sinkhole. Maybe I could make a day of it. It's not like I was needed around here.

I grabbed my comm unit too. Once I was out of earshot, I planned on calling Dr. Band. He needed to know the kind of crap I was putting up with. With any luck, he'd think the odd trio was as weird as I thought and he'd pull me off the assignment.

I walked west at first. If Lorrva or the others decided to look for me, they'd see my tracks going in the opposite direction of where they told me not to go.

Once I believed I was out of earshot, I called Dr. Band.

"How's it going?" He asked when he answered.

"Weird," I told him. "I'm barely doing anything. They're strange and secretive. I caught a peek at their lab equipment, which I'm not allowed to look at by the way, and they aren't set up to do the kind of work they told us they were doing."

"Strange." I could practically hear Dr. Band nodding and rubbing his beard on the other end.

"Yes, it's strange and it's a waste of my time. Can't you pull me out?"

"I'll do some digging and get back to you. Call if things get weirder."

True to Dr. Band fashion, he hung up before I could say anything else.

I looked around the snowy jungle in confusion. I'd walked more than half a click while I talked.

Even accounting for the wide half-circle I had to make, I should've seen signs of a sinkhole by now. I knelt down where I stood, looking for signs of any sort of disturbance in the earth.

It looked, felt, and smelled the same as the soil in the area. None of the foliage bore signs of a recent disturbance.

Why would Tovin tell me not to come here if there was no sinkhole?

A branch snapped on my left. I turned to look just as a humanoid shape darted out from between the trees. Another one followed just behind it.

"What the hell?" I cried out and leapt backward.

The human-creature-thing stood up and looked at me. It clicked to the other one. They shrieked and howled.

As I slowly backed away from them, I pulled out my comm unit and called Dr. Band.

"Maki, you haven't been there long enough to be bored yet," he answered.

The creature's eyes darted to the comm unit. They both shrieked in outrage. More came out of the trees to my right.

"What the hell was that sound?" Suddenly, he was taking the call seriously.

"I need an extraction right now!" I shouted and took off in the only direction that wasn't blocked off.

"I'm tracking your comm. Hold tight. Help is on the way."

It was difficult, but somehow, I managed to send my location without falling or dropping my comm unit.

"I'm running southwest from the last location at a full sprint," I shouted. "Please hurry."

If Dr. Band said anything back, I didn't hear him.

I risked a glance over my shoulder.

Half a dozen creatures followed me. They were eerily like the hybrids the Xathi made when they attacked cities.

Only they were different.

Whereas Xathi hybrids had crystalline skin, these creatures did not.

They looked human enough, but their movements were strange and jerky. Almost as if they weren't in complete control over their bodies.

Like they were possessed.

These creatures would chase me until either I died or they died.

I would know.

Once, I was almost one of them.

TYEHN

After I left Keith at the detention center, I sort of wandered off into the streets of Nyheim. I had refused to let Evie patch me up. Her full attention needed to be on Keith.

I had instead used some medi gel I kept in my gear. While the damage was fixed, I still looked like srell. My nose was swollen, but at least it had stopped bleeding.

Bruises covered me from head to toe, and the spot where the weight bounced off my shoulder ached terribly, but I was functional.

I was considering heading into a tavern for a stiff drink, despite the fact that I was on call.

Because what else were you supposed to do when your buddy lost his mind?

That's when my comm unit squawked, informing

me that I was being called in for duty. I heaved a heavy sigh and dutifully jogged to the armory.

Dax was on duty, probably because he'd volunteered for it.

Daxion was like that, always trying to shoulder a little more of the burden for his team. His trademark crossbow was slung across his back.

He really didn't need it in a secure building like the armory, but given all the civil unrest going on lately, I didn't blame him for wanting to be armed.

His face scrunched up with worry as I entered the armory.

"Damn, Tyehn, what the srell happened to you? You look like a Xathi gave you the once over."

"Yeah, you should see the other guy." I heaved my heavy body up to the counter and leaned on it. "I'm getting deployed to Sauma. Can you hook me up?"

Dax rubbed his palms together and grinned.

"Oh, can I ever. You want to go heavy?"

"Always. I'm the point man, after all."

"Didn't you used to be a proctologist or something?"

"Hydrologist."

He arched an eyebrow as my surly tone.

"Something wrong? Other than getting beaten, I mean."

I filled him in on the situation with Keith.

Dax knew Keith as well, and he was just as shocked as I was at his sudden, violent personality change.

"I hope he's going to be alright."

"Me, too. But what new weapons do you have for me today, Daxion?"

Dax disappeared behind the secure wall and returned a moment later with a two handed, drum fed assault rifle. My whistle of appreciation made him chuckle. Dax was not a small guy, but he had to struggle a bit to get the heavy weapon up on the counter.

"Heavy machine gun, with variable ammunition drum."

"Variable ammunition?"

"Yes. I call it the Predator."

"I'll take two."

"You'll take one and be grateful for the opportunity to wield it. It's a prototype, so try not to bust it with you ham hands."

I shouldered the rifle, feeling a lot better about things.

Maybe being a soldier had rubbed off on me over the years.

Dax gave me a half dozen extra ammo drums which I loaded into my backpack.

"I've got a side arm for you as well. Not as fancy as the predator, but you can drag it through the mud or sea and it'll still fire. And, I have one more final present."

"You honor me."

"I just feel sorry for you about the whole thing with Keith."

Dax grunted with the effort of lifting a long metal bar with a handle onto the counter. After further examination I realized it was some sort of melee weapon in a sheath.

"Is that a sword? You're giving me a sword?"

"Sword doesn't begin to cover it."

Dax unsheathed the weapon, and plucked a hair from his own scalp with a wince of pain.

"You're just lucky you're bald or I'd be doing this to you. Now watch."

He turned the blade so the sharp edge was up, and then dropped the hair. It was split neatly in two as soon as it hit the edge.

"This blade is an experimental alloy that should, given enough force behind it, cut through near anything. The sword has been sharpened to a single molecule in width, making it ridiculously sharp, so be extra careful."

"Nice."

I managed to talk Dax out of a bandoleer of hand grenades as well before we parted ways.

At that point I was running late so I ran the rest of

the way to the airfield. Sk'lar was waiting for me on the ramp, the shuttle's engines already humming.

"Move it, Tyehn, we're running late—what the hell happened to you?"

"Long story. I look like srell but I'm fit to fight."

Sk'lar seemed like he was about to argue, but it was hard to tell with those beady black eyes of his. After a moment he nodded and moved aside so I could get strapped in.

"Good. We've got an extraction request for a group of scientists out by Sauma."

The rest of Team Three noticed my bruises, but they also noticed I was in a black mood, and they didn't pry.

Which was just as well. I spent the flight to Sauma lost in thought, reliving the attack at the gym over and over in my mind.

I couldn't remember any odd smells or signs that Keith had been drugged.

Nothing.

Soon the shuttle settled in for a landing in the clearing the scientists had set up.

There were several tents there, and tons of equipment, some of which I recognized. But we didn't see anyone. The place was deserted.

"Fan out, do a quick recon of the perimeter."

We spread out as Sk'lar instructed.

I set the Predator to semi auto, and swept the barrel around in search of trouble, but didn't find any.

Cazak knelt on the snow covered jungle floor and took notice of numerous tracks.

"There's signs of at least a dozen bipeds, Commander, heading off in every direction."

"Any indications of conflict?"

"Negative. But a lot of the tracks are spread out wide, like they were running. Fast."

"Hmm." Sk'lar got that look on his face that said he was tapping in to one of his cybernetic implants, probably one that gave him enhanced vision.

A moment later he jerked around and pointed his weapon into the jungle.

"Look alive, team. We got incoming."

A moment later the unenhanced among us could also hear the approach.

Whatever it was, it wasn't bothering with stealth. We all relaxed when a human woman came through the foliage, her face oddly calm with facing off against a fully armed fire strike team.

"What's going on?" Her voice was calm, as well, but her eyes seemed wary.

"I'm Commander Sk'lar." He strode forward, but didn't offer a handshake, meaning he was feeling as wary as the rest of us. Something was out of place. "We received a distress call from your location. Is everything alright? Where is the rest of your team?"

"I'm Dr. Lorrva, the head scientist here. Everyone is out working in the jungle. I'm sorry, Commander, but I think there's been a major misunderstanding. As you can see, there's no crisis other than too much to do and not enough manpower to do it."

Sk'lar grunted and turned his back on her.

"Hang tight for a minute, Doctor. I need to speak to my team."

Sk'lar gestured for us to huddle up in a circle, our backs to Lorrva. I realized that he didn't want the scientist to hear our discussion.

"Thoughts?"

"I don't like it, Commander." Jalok shook his head and peered over at the scientist. "Something's not right here. I feel like we're being swindled, but I can't put a finger on it."

"I feel it too." Navat pursed his lips and glanced at Lorrva. "I don't trust this female."

Sk'lar spoke in an even lower tone.

"Using one of my implants, I can read the biorhythmic signature on her skin. There's something off about it, but I can't figure out what. I think she's lying, but she's damn good at it. Her heart rate didn't increase at all when she spoke."

"What are we gonna do, Commander? Bug out of

here?"

"Negative. I'm going to put in a call to Sauma and see what's up. Navat, Tyehn, and Jalok, you keep an eye on the perimeter. Don't let anything sneak up on us."

"Don't you mean anyone?"

"I meant what I said. Cazak, keep a watch on our scientist friend here. If she does anything out of the ordinary, knock her down and cuff her."

"You got it, Commander."

Sk'lar put in the call to Sauma.

He made it a conference call so the rest of us could pick it up on our comm units as we spread through the camp.

"Sauma, this is Sk'lar, do you read?"

"Read you loud and clear commander."

"What was the crisis here? Everything seems— seems normal."

He cast a suspicious glance at Lorrva when he spoke.

The comm crackled, then our contact in Sauma responded."Commander, be on high alert. Dr. Hotaru reports that she is running for base camp, being pursued by," he paused, "possessed hybrids."

"Hybrids?"

Team three and I exchanged glances.

As humans would say...the shit just hit the fan, in a big, nasty way.

MIKA

They were still behind me.

I didn't know how many. I couldn't risk taking my eyes off the forest in front of me to look.

The snow made everything harder to navigate. It disguised pitfalls, thick roots, and it was so difficult to see if there was a layer of frost or not.

My boots kept skidding on ground that looked stable but was really slippery.

"This jungle doesn't make any sense!" I groaned as I slipped once more.

This time, I slammed right into a snow-covered tree trunk. Bioluminescent frost coated my right side. It made my skin tingle but I had no time to brush it off.

Xathi hybrids were fast, inhumanly so.

I remembered.

If those creatures were some kind of variant horde that had avoided detection for all these months, I had no choice but to keep running.

My lungs burned each time I sucked in a breath. I was in damn good shape but this was pushing my limits.

My calf started cramping. Little lightning bolts of pain shot up my leg. I clenched my teeth and pushed through it.

Behind me, the creatures wailed to one another.

They flanked me.

If they caught up to me, they could close in and I didn't have any way to defend myself.

I wouldn't have the strength to fight them off bare handed after running like this.

There was something on the ground up ahead, a ripple in the snow.

As I got closer, I realized it was a sharp stone. Risking a break in my pace, I bent down and scooped it up. Thankfully, it wasn't buried in the ground.

I clutched it in my hand and waited for the creatures to cry to each other once more.

A howl sounded on my left, almost parallel to me.

There wasn't a matching one on the right. If I was correct, that meant only one of the creatures had caught up with me.

The rest couldn't be too far behind. I waited for another shriek, just to confirm my suspicions.

This time, the shriek was closer.

"Shit!"

I launched the rock without taking my eyes off the path in front of me. I heard the thump of impact and an anguished shriek.

The other creatures howled back. I heard rustling behind me. Ignoring the searing pain in my legs and lungs, I pushed myself to run faster.

The shrieks faded into the forest. The creatures must've stopped to assist their fallen member, an oddly human gesture.

Maybe they weren't Xathi hybrids, but what were they?

I took advantage and veered off the whisper-thin trail.

Almost instantly, I tripped over a log concealed by powdery snow deep enough to completely engulf me. It filled my mouth and clogged my throat. I coughed and sputtered, fighting to stick my head above the fluff.

Shrieks echoed through the forest. The creatures must've sorted themselves out and were hunting me once more.

Something moved through the tree line. It had to be one of them. I took a huge gulp of air and reburied myself in the snow. I had no other choice.

If I tried to get up and run, they would see me before I got to my feet. My legs trembled even though I wasn't standing.

If by some miracle, I managed to get to my feet before the creatures spotted me, I didn't have the strength to outrun them a second time.

I lay as still as death and waited. The snow muffled my hearing but I could still feel vibrations around me. I felt something approach. The snow shifted. Clicks and snarls sounded like they were miles above me when they were really just a few feet away. My lungs ached. I risked taking the smallest of breaths and ended up with a mouthful of snow that refused to melt.

Pain splintered between my shoulder blades. One of the creatures stood right on top of me. I willed every muscle in my body to be still. The tiniest involuntary twitch could give me away.

Tears welled in my eyes and fear formed a solid lump in my throat. I wasn't a crier. Never have been.

I didn't cry any of the five times I broke my arm.

I wasn't about to start now. But I was scared. I wasn't too proud to admit that.

I waited for the killing blow to land. Surely, the creature was just toying with me now. It knew I was here. It had to know.

Suddenly, the pressure released. The vibrations of the creature's footsteps stayed close for a few minutes then moved away. I waited as long as I could to move, but I needed air. I saw spots behind my eyelids.

I jerked my head up and took in a raspy breath filled with snow. I coughed most of it back up but I definitely swallowed some.

This was not the way I wanted to test if the snow was toxic to eat or not.

Once I wiped the powdery flakes from my eyelashes, I looked around.

I was alone in the forest. I couldn't see or hear any sign of the creatures.

After cleaning the snow off my watch, I pulled up the navigation unit. I had to get back to camp and warn the trio from hell immediately.

I wasn't a big fan of the EcoBright team but that didn't mean I wanted them torn apart by those things. Even if they were creepy, I needed their second opinion. \

A lab like EcoBright certainly would've seen the work of Dr. Evie Parr when she came up with the serum that reversed hybridism.

The serum that saved my life.

I shook my head as if I could physically shake away the memories that began to surface.

Once I was on my feet again, I took things slowly. My legs felt like jelly.

My knees barked in protest with every step. At least

walking quietly was easy with all of the snow. It muffled every twig I carelessly stepped on.

I ran in the opposite direction from camp, so the walk would take some time. I just hoped I got back to camp before the creatures found it.

I felt too tired to do anything but put one foot in front of the other. I could barely form thoughts. I certainly couldn't put the energy into listening to the forest, even though that would've helped me stay calm.

When I heard grunting sounds coming from the forest beyond, my heart nearly jumped out of my chest.

I crouched down so that I was on my belly and crawled forward through the underbrush. The grunts were louder and more plentiful as I approached. The closer I got, the less human they sounded. I must've stumbled back onto the group I just outran.

The foliage thinned a bit. I realized I was at the location where Tovin told me there'd be a sinkhole.

A sickening feeling came over me when I realized finding those creatures here instead of a sinkhole couldn't have been a coincidence.

Could it?

I knew the EcoBright team weren't fans of me or any outsiders, but I didn't think they'd send me into a trap.

If they knew about the creatures, I was sure they'd report it. They had to report it to their boss if it was a threat to the project. Whoever was behind all of this was surely pouring a ton of money into that weird little lab.

At the far end of the clearing, I could make out hunched over shapes in the snow. At first, I only saw four, but I realized there were two more, they were just wearing something white.

Coats.

Lab coats?

From a distance, they looked like humans digging frantically through the dirt and snow as if someone dropped a comm unit.

But they didn't speak. They grunted, shrieked, and clicked to one another just like the Xathi hybrids had.

They were organized, clearly searching for something.

But what?

They hadn't noticed me. I took my chance to get away. I crawled on my belly until I felt sure I wouldn't be seen if I stood up. My legs felt well enough to continue on at a light jog.

I went the long way around the area where the supposed sinkhole was supposed to be. I made it back to the camp within half an hour.

"We have a problem!" I called into the clearing.

Some new interns were milling about. They didn't look at me when I spoke.

"Hello?" I got no response. Knowing the EcoBright team leaders, the interns weren't allowed to speak until spoken to by one of them.

I wondered what exactly they were doing here for a moment but I pushed the thought away. I wasn't going to get anywhere with them. It's wasn't until I yanked back the flap of the nearest lab tent that I got anyone's attention.

"What is it about the word classified that you don't understand?" Lorrva hissed.

"Whatever sketchy shit you're up to really isn't that high on my priority list right now," I huffed back. "Did you hear me? I said we have a problem. I've been gone for over an hour!"

"Didn't notice," Tovin shrugged.

"I saw something in the jungle," I said, ignoring him. "They looked like they could've been hybrids, as in the ones the Xathi turned humans into. But they had no crystalline skin. So instead it was just like they were possessed."

"Impossible," Lorrva said a little too quickly. She wouldn't meet my gaze, but that wasn't unusual.

"Possible," I insist. "If they weren't hybrids, and not possessed, then they were definitely something. I didn't almost die getting chased by a figment of my imagination."

"Maybe you hit your head. You sound a little mad," Tovin said.

"I know what I saw. I know more about hybrids than any of you would ever want to know. If that's not convincing enough for you, at least acknowledge that I'm one of the most respected in my field and that my word isn't to be taken lightly."

"Your expertise in your field doesn't mean you can't hit your head." Tovin already went back to work on whatever it was he was working on.

I was about to argue further when I saw several big, hulking shapes standing there.

Aliens.

Specifically, a Valorni, Skotan, and K'ver.

"Who are you?" I yelped, startled.

"We're Strike Team Three," a burly alien said to me. "Who are you?"

"I'm Dr. Hotaru and I—"

Before I could continue a shriek drowned out the noise of the interns outside.

"What was that?" Lorrva looked pale.

I did my best not to look smug as we dashed out of the tent. The creatures found the camp. There were more of them now, coming at us from all directions.

"Don't argue, just run!"

TYEHN

"Spread out, team." Sk'lar gestured around the snow-covered clearing, pointing out where we should take up position. "Be ready for anything."

Lorrva kept watching us while supposedly working on her experiments. Such utter nonchalance in the face of anxiety by big, armed men was not natural or normal.

"Look alive, team, bogey coming from the left."

We sprang into action at Sk'lar's words. I could detect the crashing sounds of someone making hasty progress through the snowy jungle.

A head full of short, dark hair could be seen bobbing and weaving through the undergrowth.

In a moment he would be right on top of us. I readied the Predator and switched over to full auto.

"Going hot." I flipped the switch to explosive rounds and planted my feet wide. We could hear the sounds of many creatures tearing through the jungle, headed right for us.

But I made a mistake.

I'd forgotten about Lorrva. She suddenly bared her teeth and hissed, moving in a low, feral crouch.

It was srelling spooky.

No crystalline skin, and she'd been able to communicate with us, to try to dissuade us from investigating even.

But the jerky, movements, the blank eyes...

Possessed hybrids made as much sense as any other label.

Lorrva leaped at me, fingers splayed wide and aimed right for my eyes.

I managed to hook the barrel of the predator under her armpit and used her own momentum to hurl her head over heels to come crashing down hard on the ground.

The momentary distraction cost me dearly.

Dozens of possessed humans came rushing in, separating me from my team and surrounding us entirely.

Cursing, I switched from explosive rounds to high velocity, because of fears of collateral damage.

I squeezed the trigger and let out a deadly stream of

metal. The hail of bullets mowed down three of the possessed as they rushed in.

Their bodies jerked about, wracked with spasms as they were cut to ribbons by the heavy ordinance.

Dax wasn't kidding around with this prototype.

But they kept coming, pouring into the clearing.

Where were they all coming from?

I quickly lost count, standing my ground and sending streams of metal all about. The possessed stupidly charged on, right into the hail of bullets, dying one by one, but they didn't stop.

The pile of dead bodies grew closer and closer, and soon I knew my assault rifle would be next to useless in close quarters combat.

I considered drawing my side arm, but that would be of limited effectiveness.

With no other options, I shouldered the Predator and drew the massive molecular sword Dax gave me.

Gripping it with two hands, I swung it at the first hybrid who made it past our fire line. The blade didn't even slow down as it cleaved his head right off of his body.

I spared a quick glance for the rest of the team. I couldn't see Navat or Cazak, but Jalok was near my flank, spewing continuous death with his light rail gun.

His eyes were lit up with tiny fires, and I realized

that he was right at home dispensing doom on the battlefield.

Me, I'm a scientist first, and a soldier second.

Or at least I used to be.

I don't have much stomach for killing, and the thought that the possessed were innocent victims before their transformation weighed heavily on my mind.

Not that I stopped swinging that monster sword.

Not for a second.

Because I might have been a pacifist in an ideal world, but right now those things were trying to kill my team.

White and red, blood and snow.

All about me the formerly pristine whiteness was striped and streaked in scarlet. In an odd way I suppose it could have been beautiful, if not for the violence and the fact that we were fighting for our lives.

"Regroup to the shuttle." Sk'lar's voice held a note of strain I had not often heard from him.

The situation was bad, maybe the worst spot we'd ever been in as a team.

"We're cut off." Cazak shouted. At least he was still alive, for the time being.

"Then fight, Team Three. Fight."

Well, I didn't need Sk'lar encouragement to do that.

With renewed vigor, I swung the blade about me in

a semi circle, cleaving six of the possessed with one fell swoop.

Their bodies fell to the snow, jerking about in death throes and spraying me with more gore. The tent at my back was no longer military issue green, but a deep, rich red.

Why did they have to attack us on arm day?

My limbs began to weaken, my attacks slowed as they kept pouring into our clearing. Bodies were literally heaped up knee deep around me, and the possessed just struggled over their squirming, steaming masses to get to me.

Finally, I knew I was about to be overrun.

I switched the sword to a one handed grip and drew the predator. I switched it to full auto with my thumb and just squeezed the trigger, trying to keep my arc of fire concentrated on the clearing so as to avoid hitting my comrades.

For a time, it worked. I mowed down more of the possessed, spattering them into so much gore, and any that managed to somehow get past my deadly rain of bullets faced their doom at the hands of the molecular sword. I remember thinking at the time that if I survived, I would have to give the blade a name, too.

A sound of someone yelling reached my ears. It wasn't until my throat started to ache that I realized it was my own.

The scream was primal, guttural, the sound of an animal fighting for its very existence and deathly afraid it was losing.

We were losing. I hadn't seen any of my team for some time, though the sound of weapons fire seemed to indicate at least some of them were alive. That thought kept me going more than anything. Because if they were still alive, I still had hope.

Then the Predator ran out of standard ammo. I switched it to the toxin setting and continued to fire. The possessed didn't take well to the toxin rounds, foaming at the mouth and flopping to the ground as if they were having seizures. True to what Dax had said, the rounds also released a toxic cloud. Unfortunately, that made them as useless as explosive ordinance in close quarters.

Reluctantly, I shouldered the Predator and took my sword in a two handed grip. I was surrounded with possessed humans, closing in on me in a tight circle. I've never been too proud to retreat, and I don't make any bullshit about it being a tactical advance to the rear or any of that macho crap. But I had nowhere to run.

Then I saw something move past us in a flash.

It was the human woman who had made the initial report.

As agile and quick as a tree dwelling primate, she scampered up the trunk of a tree. I almost couldn't take in how deft and sure her movements were. She was well out of reach of the possessed, and I smiled grimly, figuring I'd at least saved one person's life even if I couldn't save myself.

The woman, Dr. Hotaru, made a mad leap for a branch and swung around it like a gymnast. She did two complete circuits before letting go and somersaulting through the frigid air.

The possessed were just as distracted by her feat as I was and watched as she spiraled towards the ground. At the last moment she untucked her body and lashed out with both feet.

She connected solidly with the back of one of the hybrid's heads, snapping his spine like a twig. Then she landed next to me and screamed at me to run.

Dr. Hotaru had opened up a gap in the circle of possessed surrounding me. I leaped past their grasping, gnashing claws and teeth and tore through the jungle after Hotaru, the possessed hot on our heels.

My long strides caught up to her and she looked at me and smiled.

Despite everything, I smiled back. She was cute and anyone who could smile in the face of danger was alright in my estimation.

Because one thing was sure.

We weren't out of it yet.

Not by a long shot.

MAKI

"What's the plan?" I shouted to the Valorni soldier as I struggled not to lose my footing in the snow.

Was it just me, or was it deeper than it was when I did this twenty minutes ago? Was there a highly-localized snow storm no one told me about?

Had anyone taken notes on this?

The overexertion was clearly going to my head.

"Run," he barked over his shoulder.

"I meant after that," I replied.

No response.

Suddenly, he veered to the right. I furrowed my brow.

Going that way lead to a ravine. The landscape was slowly but surely sloping downward. The snow was growing more plentiful and the foliage was getting lusher with each step. Most of the ravines I'd crossed so far either narrowed into a bottleneck or required climbing a steep incline to get back out of.

"Where are you going?" I shouted.

"Away from what's chasing us! Where do you think I'm going?"

"According to my navcharts it looks like right into a ravine!"

The Valorni skittered to a stop and I crashed into his broad back. It was like colliding with the side of a house.

I fell into a fluffy pile of snow. The Valorni turned around and looked down, clearly surprised to see me down there.

"What happened?"

"Did you not feel me smack into you just now?"

He offered me a hand. I stood up on my own and brushed the snow from my clothing.

"Was that what that was?"

"I can't tell if you're joking or not."

"I'll tell you when we find a safe place. Are you sure this leads to a dead end?"

"No, but it's likely. I don't want to take that chance, do you?"

A howl tore through forest.

"No, I don't. After you." He gestured toward the forest.

"Are you letting me navigate because I know the land better than you do or because you don't want to be the one who leads us into the claws of maniacs?"

"Both statements are accurate."

I held back a snort.

For a soldier, and an alien, this guy was pretty funny. If we lived through this, he'd earned an ale.

Another howl ripped through the trees bringing me back to the here and now.

"Up this way." I dash over to a rocky wall overgrown with vines and slick with frost.

"Isn't that what we were trying to avoid?"

"If I remember correctly, this levels out into a plateau. We can make a mad dash across that, come down around the other side, flip back and get my bike."

I quickly found a foothold and began my climb. It wasn't easy without my ropes and harness, but I could manage.

"That didn't make any sense but I'll take your word for it. What if there are possessed up there?"

"Then they'll eat us and it won't be our problem anymore."

"How uplifting." The Valorni pulled himself up with ease. He climbed until he was level with me, then stopped. "Would you like me to go up first? If there are possessed up there, I can fight them off better than you can."

"Sounds good," I nodded. He reached the top of the plateau while I was still struggling to get a grip on the frost covered rocks.

"We're all clear," he called down to me. "You can pick up the pace whenever you like."

"You could toss me a vine or a branch. Really, anything would be useful," I shouted back. Seconds later, a thin branch fell past me and clattered to the floor. I looked up to find a grinning Valorni.

"Very funny!"

"I thought it was. I'll go grab something to actually help you. Don't go anywhere."

I shook my head and tried to keep my laughter under control.

That alien really knew how to take the stress out of running for our lives.

Or we were both verging towards hysterical.

Either way, it worked for me.

My foot kept slipping off its hold. If I timed this wrong, I'd fall.

I was less than ten feet off the ground, so falling was unlikely to injure me but it would cost us valuable time.

Clicks and shrieks rose from the trees behind me as the possessed burst forward. They glared up and me and bared their teeth.

"How's it going with that branch, buddy?"

One of the possessed made a leap for my leg. I kicked out, making contact with his jaw. He reeled back and let out a rage-filled scream.

"It's Tyehn."

A woven braid of vines plopped down next to me.

"Are you going to grab it or stare at it?"

I took hold of the vine rope with one hand and kept the other hand on the rock. Tyehn pulled slowly until I found a good climbing rhythm.

He took my elbow when I was close enough and hauled me over.

The possessed tried to climb as well, but they couldn't keep their footing on the frosty rocks.

"What's the next step of your up, over, back and around plan?" Tyehn asked as we hurried away from the edge of the plateau.

"That plan puts us back on an even footing with those things," I shuddered. "New plan."

"Which is?"

"A plan that's new."

"And the weight's been lifted from my shoulders." Tyehn's voice dripped with sarcasm.

I waved him off. "Give me a moment to think."

Before I could come up with a brilliant lifesaver of a plan, more shrieks echoed through the forest.

"Srell! How many more of them are there?" Tyehn groaned.

"At this point, we should assume everyone who isn't us is one of them."

We took off jogging in the opposite direction of the shrieks and wails.

"Those possessed at the bottom of the ledge couldn't climb, right?" Tyehn asked.

"The frost on the rocks made it too slippery for them."

"And for you."

"We're not talking about me."

"Right. Let's look for another ledge for me to help you climb. That'll put another level between us and the possessed."

"The elevation changes aren't that drastic here. I don't think we'll find another one." I tripped over another damn root and caught myself on a tree trunk. Unfortunately, it was covered in frost. I lost my grip and slipped forward.

Tyehn's hand shot out and wrapped around my forearm.

"I can't tell if you're good at this or not," he said.

"I'm not wearing footwear that does well in snow! They don't sell any in Sauma because it's Sauma! We don't do snow."

"Whatever you say." Tyehn laughed and released my arm.

"Wait, you just gave me an idea. Can you make another one of those vine ropes?"

"Coming right up." I could tell Tyehn was confused but he didn't question me. He grabbed some hanging vines from the tree and wove them together.

"Will that hold your weight?" I asked.

"Why?"

"Because we're climbing." I pointed up to the canopy.

"Worry less about the vines holding me. Worry more about the branches holding me."

"We'll deal with that when we get to it." I grabbed the vines and started climbing up the frosty tree trunk, trailing the makeshift rope behind me.

"That's a terrible plan."

"If you can think of a better one before I find a comfy branch, we'll go with your idea. Until then, up we go."

Tyehn waited until I situated myself on a narrow branch near the top of the tree. I left the thickest branches open for him to choose from.

"That one looks like it'll hold you." I pointed to a branch beneath mine on the opposite side of the trunk.

"You realize my bones are eight times denser than

yours? I grew up on a planet with gravity so heavy it would crush your little bones."

"How would I know anything about your bones? Just pick a branch before the horde shows up."

Tyehn gingerly sat on a branch, clinging to the vine rope like a lifeline. The branch didn't even bend under his weight.

"Looks like the branch can handle those thick bones of yours just fine," I smirked and shimmied down to be on level with him.

"I didn't say thick. I said dense."

"Do your dense bones have a plan?"

"Shh." Tyehn raised his hand to silence me.

A scurrying sound came from beneath us. Possessed roamed between the trees. They were clearly searching for something but they weren't in pursuit.

If I didn't look at them too closely, I'd think they were just normal people out for a stroll.

But they weren't.

We waited in tense silence until the horde moved on.

Once we were sure they were far enough away, I let out a sigh of relief.

"Our best bet is to make it to an outpost or a shuttle," Tyehn said.

"I've got a bike that can get us there but it's back at the camp."

"Too risky. The possessed liked your camp, remember? Besides, if they're anything like the ones the Xathi created, they might've turned some of the other scientists."

"You're right." I chewed on my bottom lip and tried to think of something. "I just really like that bike."

"I'll figure out a way to get your bike." Tyehn rolled his eyes. "I'll call in an evac for it if you want."

"Would you?"

"I was joking but you genuinely look like you're about to weep. If it comes to it, I'll make sure you get it back."

"I'm not about to weep." I straightened up. "But thank you."

"You don't need to thank me. Just admit that a bike brought you to tears."

"I will push you off that branch. How hard will your land with those thick bones of yours?"

"Dense."

"Yes, you are." I grinned.

"Very funny." He shot me a look before pulling out some kind of alien contraption.

"Can that thing teleport us or is that too wishful?"

"If I had something capable of teleporting us, don't you think I would've used it sooner?"

"Fair point. Can't blame me for hoping. What is it, then?"

"A navigation unit. It'll tell us how to get to the nearest shuttle stop."

"It can't detect nearby possessed, can it?"

"We aren't that lucky. Come on." Tyehn scooted off his branch and dropped to the ground, landing on his feet.

"I can't do that," I called down after him. "I'm human."

"Don't worry. I don't hold that against you," he grinned up at me. I pursed my lips and grabbed the vine rope. I wrapped my legs around it and slid down to the ground.

"Not bad for a human, right?"

"Ask me that again once we make it out of here alive."

TYEHN

Night descended on the jungle, turning the winter wonderland into a place darker than the deepest cave.

Maki—it seemed odd to call her Dr. Hotaru now, after the experience we'd shared—walked a pace ahead of me.

We lost the pursuing possessed earlier.

They seemed to have been confused by our hiding spot, so at least we weren't dealing with enhanced senses like smell.

The darkness made our going difficult, but since the horde didn't seem to have night vision, it hampered them, as well.

Maki unexpectedly stopped, and I stepped on the back of her heel. She yelped, far too loud for the circumstances, and hissed in recrimination for both my clumsiness and her noise.

"Watch where you're going, you lumbering killing machine."

"Sorry. Can't see a damn thing here."

"Hold my hand, then. I'll lead you along the path."

"Uh, okay."

I awkwardly reached out into the darkness for her hand.

Unfortunately, I'd forgotten how much taller I was than Maki. My fingers closed around something soft and pliant, and she shrieked, then slapped my chest.

"That's not my hand."

"Sorry."

Much more carefully, and at the right height, I reached for her in the darkness. Her fingers clutched at my much larger limb and snagged securely.

"My fingers don't even fit around your hand. You're huge."

"That's just a rumor made up by human women."

She chuckled softly in the darkness.

"I should slap you again for that comment."

"Shouldn't you be wearing leather first?"

"Maybe, but you have to buy me some drinks first."

"If we make it back to civilization alive, I'll buy you a whole bar."

The banter helped to dispel some of our nervous energy.

Not all, but a bit.

The last thing we wanted to talk about was the fact that we were in huge trouble.

We'd been cut off from Team Three, my comm unit was damaged in our fleeing that we were only able to transmit in very short ranges, and we were being stalked by some sort of hybrids that were no longer supposed to exist on this planet.

Part of me wondered if we could appeal to the Puppet Master, but I had no idea of how to do it.

Jalok had communicated with him before. Though, according to Jalok, the Puppet Master had initiated the contact.

I guess when you're a massive planet sized being the troubles of a few of the germs crawling over your skin don't get your attention much.

Maki's hand seemed so tiny inside of my own.

But I remembered the way she moved back during the assault at the camp site, and I knew that she could take care of herself.

This was no damsel in distress, and I was glad for that.

Unfortunately, it had been a srell of a long day for me. First I'd worked out hard, trying to outdo Keith.

Then Keith had attacked me in the gym and bruised

me up pretty good. After that, I'd first run to the armory and then to the airfield.

Then there was the brutal fight at the camp, and the desperate run through the jungle afterward.

And there was no getting around the hard facts. "I'm getting tired."

"I am too." Maki's voice was soft. "We should find a place to rest for the night."

The idea of falling asleep on the jungle floor didn't sit very well with me at all.

"You know this area better than I do. Are there any caves, or any type of shelter we could use?"

"No, I don't know of any caves in this area that won't be flooded with the recent precipitation. But I have an idea."

She stopped ahead of me, and I nearly bumped into her again. I waited for a few moments but she didn't budge.

"Ah, you said you had an idea?"

"Oh, shit, I'm pointing up right now. I forgot you can't see me."

"Up? What, you want us to fly?" I laughed at the notion. "I can flap my arms real hard but I don't think we'll get much altitude."

She had the good grace to laugh at my lame joke.

"Fly, no, but I think we can climb."

"Climb, huh? That might work, if you think you can find another tree sturdy enough to hold me."

"I know of just the one. It's an ancient growth with a trunk so thick your entire Strike Team could hold hands and not reach around to the other side."

The mention of team Three made me worry again about Sk'lar and the others.

If they'd managed to stay together, they'd be fine. But separated, it was far too easy to pick us off one by one.

And without a working comm unit...

I hoped they were all right, but things seemed pretty bleak.

Maki led us to the tree in question, and even in the dark it was imposing. It appeared as a massive black hulk darker than the surrounding shadows. The only problem was that the trunk was sheer, and the lowest branch dangled a full thirty feet off the forest floor.

"Damn." Maki sighed. "I guess this won't do after all. C'mon, let's go find another one."

"Wait." I resisted the light tug of her hand when she tried to lead me on. "I can get us up there. But you'll have to climb onto my back."

"Oh boy, why do I get the feeling that I'm not going to like this one bit?"

We spent a few minutes using some of the jungle vines to rig up a makeshift safety harness that went over my shoulders, under my armpits and tied at my sternum.

Maki climbed under the vines and slithered up onto my back. Her body was warm, shielding me from the chill jungle wind.

"Okay, I'm secure back here. What are you going to do? Can your species jump like Skotan do?"

"I'm afraid not, but I can climb."

"There aren't any handholds."

"I'll make some."

I dug my fingers into the bark until they sank in. Then, hand over hand, I dragged the two of us up to the lowest branch.

Even though she was secured by the vines, Maki clung to my back tightly.

We finally made it up to the branch, and from there she was able to get herself up. It was a good thing, too, because at that point I was nearing total exhaustion.

Using some more vines, we managed to rig something akin to a hammock for the two of us. Because of the tight confines of our thrown together shelter, and the cold, we had to huddle together.

I didn't mind, though.

Her body pressing against mine was oddly pleasing.

Or maybe not so odd. My body responded to her warmth in ways that were wildly inappropriate.

Fortunately, I had a lot of other thoughts to distract myself with.

Maki soon fell asleep, snoring softly into my chest. I remained awake, troubled by memories stirred up by the possessed.

When the Xathi war had first ravaged the Valorni homeworld, I'd seen a loving mother turned into one of those things. She'd attacked her own children.

Her children.

If I hadn't been there, she'd have ripped them to shreds without a modicum of mercy or remorse.

We'd barely been able to save the kids, but the mother had run off into the forest, and the fighting had moved on.

I had no idea what had happened to her.

Here on Ankou, all of the Xathi hybrids were supposed to have been cured by Evie's serum, but what if some had stayed hidden?

Would that be better or worse than some sort of new crises?

My thoughts circled endlessly. I was definitely glad to have run into Maki, and not just because she saved my ass.

Her sense of humor was a treasure in dark times, quite similar to my own in a lot of ways. Not only that, but I couldn't help but admire her physical form.

Lean and quick and lithe, she was like the exact opposite of myself.

After a time, I did finally manage to drift off for some much needed sleep.

I had no idea how long we slumbered, but the sun was well over the horizon when I awakened.

Maki was already alert, and when I started to speak she put her finger on my lips and pointed down at the jungle floor.

I peered through the foliage and saw a group of possessed searching the area below.

They must have followed our tracks.

Relentless. Whatever they were, they weren't human anymore. Humans couldn't have kept up that pace, searching for all those hours.

We were forced to spend another two hours shivering up in the tree, and trying not to think about how badly we needed to pee. Just when my bladder was on the verge of bursting, the possessed all snorted and took off at a dead run, leaving us alone at last.

Maki wanted to wait a little longer—it seems like females of any species can hold their urine longer—but I had had enough of the tree by that point.

I clambered down with her on my back, and gratefully, we both went off in separate directions to relieve ourselves.

Once we'd somewhat pulled ourselves together, she spoke.

"What are we going to do? It's many miles to the edge of the jungle on foot, and those things are roaming all over the place."

"We need to get back to the shuttle. It's our best chance."

Assuming it's still there, and if so, that it can still fly.

I could tell Maki was worried about that as well, but she was quiet, just gnawed at her lip.

But we had little choice, so we trudged off wearily toward the camp.

And kept our concerns to ourselves, and our eyes peeled for trouble.

"You're quiet all of a sudden," Tyehn said as we walked through the snowy jungle.

"I'm just listening."

"Why are you walking with your eyes closed? You've tripped over at least ten roots since we left the camp."

"Like I said, I'm listening," I repeated.

"I'd feel better if you listened with your eyes open. Never thought I'd have to specify that." Tyehn sounded like he was shaking his head, not that I could tell by his voice.

I wasn't that talented.

However, if our situations were reversed, I'd be shaking my head.

"That's not how it works." I decided to toy with him

a little bit. It kept the mood light and the adrenaline in check.

"Please explain to me how listening works. One of us has a fundamental misunderstanding and I don't think it's me."

"I close my eyes so that I can concentrate more on what I hear. You'd be amazed at the difference it makes," I explained. "Don't try it now, though. One of us needs to be able to see where we're going."

"That's exactly what you would say if you were feeding me a load of srell," Tyehn tutted.

"It takes practice to be able to truly listen. When the Xathi war ended, I had a lot of issues I needed to work through. Learning how to breathe again was the first step. Learning how to see was the second. Finally, I had to relearn how to listen. Lucky for me, my father taught me how to listen to the world around me when I was very young. It wasn't hard to relearn how to do this correctly."

"I'm sorry." He was no longer teasing me. I heard genuine remorse in his voice. "It's not my place to judge how anyone copes after the Xathi war."

"You don't have anything to apologize for. I wasn't offended." I listened to his footsteps and figured out where he was in relation to me. I reached out and patted his shoulder.

"What were you aiming for?"

"Your shoulder. Why?"

"You did not touch my shoulder. That was my chest."

"Oh." I felt a blush on my cheeks, though I didn't know why. "Sorry."

"Don't apologize. You didn't offend me," he shot my line back at me. "What are you listening for, again?"

"Listening keeps me from panicking. Also, if I'm extremely focused, I'm better at feeling the vibrations of other creatures. Might be helpful since we're trying to outrun a horde of possessed."

"You don't seem focused."

"I'm not but that's not going to stop me from trying."

My foot caught on something on the ground. Probably another damned root. I didn't panic as I stumbled forward.

My hand went to the nearest tree to stop my fall, but not before two strong hands gripped my shoulders.

"It's time to open your eyes."

My lids fluttered open. I found myself looking up at Tyehn. He looked equal parts concerned and amused.

"Much better." He had a handsome smile. I felt another blush coming so I straightened myself up and stepped back.

"Thanks. I would've caught myself, you know?"

"I'm sure of it." He winked. "Did you hear anything interesting?"

"Yes, actually. Aside from our chatter, I heard nothing."

"How is that interesting?" Tyehn made a show of crushing down a wayward root so I could pass over it without tripping.

"How much time have you spent in the forests of Ankou?" I asked.

"Too much," he laughed.

"When has it ever been this silent?"

Tyehn's smile dropped as he listened to what neither of us were hearing.

"That's not normal."

"No," I sighed. "It's not. All of the creatures are hiding or have moved somewhere else. That's never a good sign."

"Could that also mean the possessed have moved on to a more active part of the forest?" I considered this for a moment.

"It's possible," I agreed. "I wouldn't bet my life on it."

A beep came from Tyehn's comm unit.

"Maybe you should. Look."

He showed me a tiny console screen with a little green dot.

"Is that supposed to mean something to me?"

"That's the shuttle station at the EcoBright camp,"

Tyehn explained. "It was offline all day but now it's back on."

"It must be running now. The EcoBright team must've sent the shuttle for evacuations."

"Let's go see if they need any help. Walk with your eyes open this time, please?" Tyehn chuckled. We picked up a steady running pace and made it back to the camp within the hour.

There was no sign of the EcoBright team but the shuttle was there. It had been tipped on its side and completely gutted.

"This doesn't look recent," I frowned. "I thought the signal just went off?"

"It did. I don't understand."

"We'll just have to be careful," I said.

Tyehn let out a groan of frustration.

"Well, my bike's just over there. I don't think it's been messed with." I tapped his arm and wave for him to follow me.

Ever since I'd been assigned to the EcoBright team, I'd been parking my bike just outside of the clearing.

Luckily, it was exactly where I left it and untouched by the possessed.

"You're kidding right?" Tyehn laughed when he saw it. "I'm never going to fit on that."

"It's stronger than it looks," I replied. "The bike was

custom made for my height but it can hold much more than my weight."

"How much more?"

"Not sure. Let's give it a go. That shuttle's not taking us anywhere anytime soon. It's been damaged."

I swung into the seat and patted the space behind me.

"That's not even six inches of space," Tyehn laughed.

"Stand on the supports here. Don't sit. We can make this work."

"Your optimism's impressive. I'll give you that much."

Tyehn swung his leg over the bike and tried to find a place that would work. He was so tall that my back rested against his thighs when he stood on the back of the bike. The bike groaned under the weight of us.

I used the hand scanner to power it up. It rumbled to life but it didn't sound right. When I slowly pushed the lever to move it forward, it refused to budge.

"This isn't going to work," I sighed.

"That's what I told you." He swung his leg back over and stepped away from the bike. "You should take it and ride out of here. I'll find a way back."

"That's not fair," I said. "I'll walk the bike out with you. We shouldn't split up with those things still out there."

"I'm giving you a chance to get out of here faster. Take it."

"How about this? If worst comes to worst, I'll ditch you on the bike."

"Perfect," he grinned. "Let's take one more look at the shuttle before we head out. Maybe we can get it running."

"I'm game if you are."

Together, we walked my bike over to the upturned shuttle.

"The signal transmitter is still in one piece." Tyehn picked up a hunk of metal with a green flashing light. "Why wasn't it activated before?"

The telltale shrieks of the possessed tore our attention from the shuttle.

"You don't think they activated the shuttle signal to lure someone in, right?" I asked.

"No. That would be ridiculous." Tyehn sounded as unconvinced as I felt.

"Right. That would mean they're capable of advanced planning."

"We're in deep srell, aren't we?"

"Only if we stick around. And... there's something I need to tell you."

I pushed my bike behind the shuttle and hoped that would be enough to stop it from getting torn to pieces when the possessed arrived.

"Tell it to me fast, and get out of here, Maki," Tyehn growled.

"The bike's not running at all. The signal transmitter is on, but it's like the power cells have been drained."

"Seriously?"

I canted my head. "Would I joke at a time like this?"

"Yes," he deadpanned.

No sooner had I taken my place next to Tyehn than the possessed burst forward from the tree line.

"I'm so sick of this," I groaned. "Which way's the nearest outpost?"

"Southwest of us, I think. First step, getting the hell out of here."

The possessed clicked and chittered to each other as they fanned out around us. A few hunched forward, ready to lunge at the perfect moment.

I was determined not to give them that moment.

"I'm not keen on taking my eyes off those things to check my navigation unit," Tyehn snapped.

"Fair enough. Southwest it is. On my signal." I lifted a hand and bid him to follow my lead. As the possessed moved, I mirrored their movements. I angled myself so that I faced southwest.

"Run!" I shouted.

We took off toward the tree line with the possessed on our heels.

"How many more times am I going to have to do this today?" I groaned.

Tyehn kept pace with me but as the possessed started gaining on us, he moved faster.

"Pick up the pace!" He called back to me.

"This is as fast as I can go." Already my legs were burning from overexertion.

"You should've taken your bike."

"Believe me, I wish it was an option" I was only half joking. Up ahead, I spied a low hanging branch.

One of the horde lunged at me, missing my leg by half an inch. Without hesitation, I leapt for the low branch and used my momentum to push me forward to the next one.

"What are you doing?" Tyehn shouted from below me.

"Outrunning psychotic monster-people," I replied. "Swing up on the next low branch you see then follow my lead."

I leaped far enough to pass Tyehn below me. I couldn't take my eyes off the path of branches, vines, trunks, and boulders in front of me to check on him but I heard him swing up before long.

When I had a moment of stability, I looked back.

Tyehn threw himself from landing spot to landing spot. He wasn't properly balanced and relied entirely on his strength to keep himself from falling, but now wasn't the time to critique his form.

As long as he didn't fall to his death, we were fine.

"Now I'm really wishing you took the bike," he yelled to me.

"I'm not. This is way too fun. Now, pick up the pace!"

TYEHN

"What you moping about up there?" Maki asked me as we kept going.

I looked down at her and couldn't help but be impressed by how resilient she was considering how tiny she was compared to me.

"I'm not moping," I answer, putting on a pouty face to emphasize my point.

She laughed. "Yeah, okay there jolly green giant. If you're not moping, then I'm flying in the sky right now."

"I can make that happen, you know," I quipped back. "But, in seriousness, I'm not moping, just thinking. I'm trying to figure out how these people are becoming hybrids again."

"Yeah," she nodded. "It does seem a bit odd since there aren't any Xathi left."

"That's exactly what I was thinking," I answer as I grabbed my canteen and offered it to her. She accepted it and took a hard pull from it.

"Thanks," she said as she handed it back to me. I nodded in return as I took a healthy pull myself.

"Any idea what direction we're headed?" I asked as we crunched through more snow. I looked up to see a few more flakes falling, but the tree cover was catching most of it, for now.

"Honestly? No," she answered me. "Sika's not a big jungle, but she also doesn't follow most jungle rules either. There's no moss on the trees and with the cloud cover right now, can't see the sun."

I nodded as I stepped over a fallen tree, reaching back to offer her help. She took my hand and smiled a thank you to me as she climbed over it.

It wasn't a big tree, but she was forced to climb thanks to her lack of height.

"You had to climb," I teased her with a forced chuckle.

"Shut up," she responded with a slap to my arm. "We can't all have mile long legs like your lanky ass."

I held back my chuckle and simply responded with a "Ah, jealous of the legs, huh."

She shrugged a little. "Nah, always liked my height.

Makes it easier to get in and out of things. Plus, I don't have to worry about hitting my head on things like doorways or branches, look out."

I immediately ducked as I stepped forward. I looked back and saw that there was a good sized branch where my face would have been. "Thank you. Not sure how that meeting with the tree would have worked out for me."

"Probably not well." She smiled up at me as we walked and I found myself drawn into that smile, like a planet into a black hole.

I fought it, but I could tell I was losing the battle.

"True," I smiled back at her. We continued making our way through, at a slow pace thanks to the increasing snow fall. "I wonder if anyone can follow our trail?" I say as I looked back and took notice of the massive footprints I was leaving in the snow next to Maki's smaller ones.

She looked back. "Nah, we're invisible. Those are animal tracks."

"Makes sense. You were snoring like one last night," I said just as I jumped forward to avoid the inevitable smack.

"Hey!" I looked back to see her mouth agape in exaggerated shock. "You weren't exactly quiet yourself."

"Quiet enough to keep the possessed away," I shot back. "Thirsty?"

"Wait, what?"

"I'm asking if you're thirsty."

"A little. Why?"

I looked down at my boots as I stood in the small stream that I had accidentally jumped into. "No reason," I answered.

As she approached, she had a knowing look on her face. "Ah, you found water, and as usual, you had to go and step in it, didn't you?"

I put my arms out to my side. "I was trying to make sure it was safe, and since it's not burning my boots, we know it's water and not a stream of acid."

I watched as she tried to hold back the laughter, but she failed miserably. I took out my canteen, drank a bit, then handed to her to finish off.

After she emptied it, I refilled it from the stream. It was ice cold, which wasn't surprising considering the weather.

I heard a rustling noise and looked back to see her opening a pack of what looked to be dried fruit. She held it out to me with a questioning look on her face.

"Thank you," I said as I cupped my hand. She poured some into my palm, then dipped her fingers into the pack and ate some.

I took a few pieces out and put them in my mouth, letting my saliva rehydrate them before chewing on them. I was pleasantly surprised by the rush of flavor that was still there.

Dried food, outside of what the humans called beef jerky, was not one of my more pleasant memories here.

"What do we do now?" she asked after a few minutes.

I shrugged as I put the rest of the fruit into my mouth. After a minute of chewing, I finally had an empty enough mouth to answer.

"I'm not sure. We keep walking and hope we either reach the end of the jungle so we can figure out where we are, or we make it back to the shuttle. Hopefully my team will be there, in one piece, and we'll be able to get out of here."

"Okay. What if we don't make it to the shuttle and end up leaving the jungle instead?" she asked as she pulled out another pack of dried fruit.

"Then we figure out a new plan from there," I answered. "Don't worry, I'll do everything that I can to keep you safe."

"Yeah? With what? I think you're out of ammunition there, Jolly."

I flashed her a look when she called me 'Jolly,' but I chose to ignore it for the moment. "I still have some ammunition, plus my sword and my knives. If all else fails, I make you talk to them and we should be fine."

"Oh, o-o-okay. You find me that annoying then," she stated.

I throw my arms out wide as I put on an over-exaggerated thinking face. "No, not annoying per se," I dragged out the last syllable.

With a gasp of indignation, she reached down and grabbed some snow to throw at me. Her 'weapon' went wide. "You throw like a human," I teased.

"I'll show you 'human'," she shot back as she grabbed more snow, taking her time to pack it tight. I stood there, on the edge of the stream, waiting.

As she stood and threw, I barely dodged it. She could throw. As I stood up, another snowball hit me in the chin and she erupted into laughter.

"Nice," I said as I wiped the snow away. "Good throw."

"Thank you," she returned with a curtsey.

I shook my head and smiled. "I'll be right back, need to answer nature."

"Gross, but thanks for letting me know you'll be back," she grimaced.

I walked a few paces away and went behind a tree to relieve myself. There was something different about this woman from all of the others that I knew.

She could most certainly take care of herself if needed, and she seemed to be unafraid of anything, except the things she needed to be afraid of.

Even then, it didn't seem as though she was scared, just appropriately cautious and aware of the situation. She seemed to know when running was a good idea.

She's a Valorni in human skin, I started to think to myself as I finished. I was cut short by Maki's scream.

In less than two seconds, I was back where Maki was.

She was surrounded by six possessed.

These ones looked different than the ones we fought in the clearing.

They weren't dressed like scientists or the team of guards they had with them.

They looked like normal people, one of them was even in a business-style suit while another looked to be some sort of cook or something from a restaurant.

They might be every day, regular people, except for one thing.

They were closing in on Maki.

Primal rage took over and I let out a growl that made them all jump.

I didn't remember moving, but I was suddenly in the middle of them all, tearing, punching, breaking, and kicking at anything that wasn't Maki.

One of them jumped on my back, but I punched back and felt the sickening, yet oddly satisfying feeling of a face crushing beneath my blow.

As the body fell from my back, I kicked out at one

that was reaching out for Maki while she kicked another one twice in the knee and once in the head without her foot ever touching the ground.

"Impressive," I grunted out as I picked her up and started running.

My longer legs helped us put distance between ourselves and the possessed before I put her down and we started running again, my own pace slowing to match hers.

MAKI

"Go! We've got to move," Tyehn barked.

"Can you walk?" I asked.

We'd made it out of the first fight unscathed.

Not the second. A lucky strike by one of the mob had cut into his side, leaving a nasty gash.

A hybrid lunged at him. I grabbed a stick and jabbed it into the hybrid's arm with all of my strength. It let out a shriek and whirled on me.

Tyehn kicked it square in the back and stomped on its neck when it fell.

"If I can do that, I can do more than walk." He grinned at me. I could tell he was trying to keep the mood light but I saw the pain behind his eyes, clear as day.

We needed to stop and get him patched up. Between us, we had the supplies.

But we didn't have the time.

"If you say so. Let's go." I took off at an easy jog, letting him set the pace. He grunted with each step, clearly favoring one side.

"Are you sure you're alright?" I asked again.

"Stop worrying. Just get ahead." He waved me forward with his free hand. Even that motion seemed to cause him pain. I slowed down and allowed him to catch up.

"I'm not leaving you behind if that's what you're getting at." I placed my hands firmly on my hips. "We're in this together now. You're going to have to deal with that."

"You're going to have to deal with me. I'm too much of a burden. I can handle myself but I can't look after you, as well, like this."

"Look after me?" I chuckled. "That won't be a problem. Have you been paying attention for the last few hours?"

Howls rose from the forest. The hybrid horde was going to find us sooner rather than later if we didn't move now.

"Come on." I lined myself up next to him and offered my arm. He linked his free arm through mine.

"You can't support me," he laughed.

"After everything you've seen me do since we met, how can you still doubt me?"

"It's not a reflection of your abilities. Dense bones, remember?"

"Right. We'll let's give it a go. If we stumble and fall it's-"

"No longer our problem?"

"That's the spirit." My laugh came out more like a cough. Tyehn shifted some of his weight onto me. My legs immediately buckled.

"Fucking hell." I grabbed a low hanging branch for support.

"What did I tell you?"

"I know, I know." I waved my hand dismissively. "We've got to come up with something. The horde will be on top of us any moment now."

Tyehn looked around. His gaze settled on the tree I clung to. He ran his fingers over the trunk.

"This one isn't as slippery as the last. What's the phrase you humans like? The one about broken things?"

"If it ain't broke, don't fix it?" I guessed.

"That's the one. The trees kept us safe the first time so why not a second?"

"How are you going to climb if you can barely run?" I asked.

"We'll figure that out when we get to it," he shrugged.

"That phrase doesn't work if we're already at the thing we need to deal with."

"I'm trying to make this fun."

"It's a near death experience. It's already fun," I grinned. Tyehn gave me a strange look.

"You're nothing like any of the other humans I've interacted with."

"I'm going to take that as a compliment," I decided. "Can you fight if the possessed show up?"

"I have a personal blaster left, so yes," he nodded.

"Good. Stay here. I'm going to climb up and get some vines. I think that's the only way to get you up there."

Tyehn was right. There wasn't as much frost on this tree as there was on the last one. I was able to climb up high enough to reach some sturdy looking vines. They were all in a tangled mess. With a sigh, I started to detangle them.

This was going to take far too long. But I wasn't leaving him behind.

Not a chance.

Tyehn's blaster went off, startling me.

"What was that?" I called down to him. "Are you okay?"

"I'm fine," Tyehn called back with a proud grin on his face. "He's not."

He gestured to the body of one of the horde laying in the snow about one hundred yards away.

Nothing looked amiss, except for the part where it was missing a head. Chunks of it were strewn across the snow.

"Nice shot." I nodded with approval.

"Thank you. How's it going over there? Are you having a go at making a rope?"

"I've got this." I whipped the single length of untangled vine in his direction.

He grabbed it and looked back up at me with a smirk.

"Don't think this is going to work."

"I worked that one out for myself, thanks," I called back. "For someone who's losing an alarming amount of blood, you're very quippy."

"It helps me deal with the pain. Have you tried this?" Tyehn gave the vine a sharp tug hard enough to dislodge the tangle of vines.

They unfurled gracefully into a waterfall of lush greenery.

"No, I haven't tried that."

Tyehn took a fist full of vines and started hauling himself up.

"Can you manage?" I bit my lip as I watched him climb.

"I have to, don't I?" He grunted back.

"How can I help?"

"Keep watch while I concentrate. I'm too heavy for you to pull up."

"Maybe not." I looked at the vines and at the surrounding branches. "Hold on tight. I have an idea."

I wiggled down to a lower branch and looped some vines over the thickest one I could find.

"Grab these." I shook the looped vines. Tyehn gave me a skeptical look but did it anyway. I grabbed the other ends of the vines, took hold and slowly started to lean back.

"In order for that to work, you need to weigh more than me," Tyehn called.

I leaned so far back that I was parallel to the ground. Tyehn hadn't budged an inch.

"Damn you and your dense bones."

"I appreciate the effort." His laughter was cut short by the clicks and howls of approaching possessed.

They were on the hunt, and they were getting closer.

"Can you see them?" Tyehn asked quietly once I'd climbed back into an upright position. He resumed his slow placed climb with renewed vigor.

"Yes. They've found their headless friend."

Tyehn threw his arm over a branch and used the trunk for leverage.

"I can't climb any higher," he whisper-shouted. "I'll lose too much blood and waste too much energy."

I swung down to the lower branches to be on his level.

"Any ideas?" I asked.

"Look," he jerked his chin toward the cluster of possessed. They sniffed and kicked at their headless horde member nervously. "They know something killed their troop mate. With a little luck, their need to survive will outweigh their need to hunt."

I didn't say anything, but I knew that it wasn't likely.

The need to fulfill the hunt was all consuming.

They were daunted by the body of the other hybrid now, but they would get over it.

The question was how much time did we have until then?

"We need to come up with a plan. Now."

"This is the plan."

"We need a better one. Can't you call for an extraction or something?"

"The other units are on their own missions. However, I might be able to do something."

I watched the possessed as they continued to investigate the body.

I hated watching them. Just looking at them sent chills down my spine and made me feel sick to my stomach.

I closed my eyes to block out the painful memories that started to surface.

I could still feel it, that need to hunt and obey.

"Are you ill?" Tyehn asked softly.

"No," I said too quickly. "Just tired. And starving. How's that plan coming?"

"Signal's still weak out here." He lifted his arm to show me his complex alien watch-thing. "I've been trying to get through to the command center back in Nyheim but the comm was damaged earlier."

"Hurry up." I didn't mean to sound so harsh.

I just needed to get out of here. Tyehn looked at me, his eyes filled with concern.

Funny, since he was the one with a gash in his gut.

Thankfully, he said nothing and continued trying to get in touch with Nyheim.

One of the possessed lifted his head, searching. He sniffed the air then bent down to sniff the snow and earth.

He could smell us.

He clicked to the others letting them know of his discovery.

This tree wasn't covered in as much frost as the last one.

The possessed might be able to climb up if we didn't move fast enough.

"This is Strike Team Three member Tyehn

requesting to be put through the Aurora member Fen," Tyehn whispered into this comm unit.

"Speak up soldier. We're unable to hear your request." Whoever's voice was on the other end came through loud and clear. Every hybrid looked in our direction. They started shrieking.

"Damn it!" I groaned. "Climb if you can. They've found us."

Tyehn repeated his request at a shout.

"You're unauthorized to make that request," the command center replied.

"Just do it! A civilian's life is at risk. I'm injured. We need a rift extraction."

"What's that?" I asked.

The possessed circled the trunk of our tree. They clicked and chittered to each other as if discussing which one of them would try to climb it first.

"Speak." A woman's voice came through Tyehn's comm unit.

"Fen, I've sent you my location. Please open a rift. It's a matter of life and death."

"Don't blame me if you get in trouble," she replied.

"This is going to be cold," Tyehn warned me.

"What are you talking about?" I hadn't taken my eyes off the possessed.

"This." Tyehn grabbed my arm. I looked up to find a

shimmering portal of blue light suspended in the air in front of us.

"What the hell is that?" I exclaimed.

"Our escape plan."

"That looks like a death sentence," I argued.

"No, that looks like a death sentence." Tyehn looked beneath me.

I followed his gaze. One of the possessed had clawed its way up the tree without me noticing. It was only one branch beneath us.

"Shit!"

Tyehn wrapped his arm around my waist and launched us toward the portal just as the hybrid lunged for us.

TYEHN

We hit the ground, hard.

That wasn't surprising considering how for up we were when we entered the rift.

Maki was on top of me, shivering uncontrollably. I had warned her, but then I didn't even give her a chance to prepare for the rift before pulling her through it.

"Are you okay?" I asked.

She nodded, but I wasn't sure if she did so because she was okay or because she was just making sure she could still move.

"Hey, look at me," I ordered.

She stopped shivering to stare into my eyes.

"You've just gone through a rift. It's a way of

traversing from one place to another very quickly. I'm sorry that had to be your first way through one."

"Where are we?"

I looked at her with squinted eyes, then took a second to assess the situation.

I didn't see sky above her, I saw earth. This wasn't grass and snow under me, it was dirt. "Where in the hell are we?"

"I just asked you that," she sighed as she rolled off of me. She wasn't shivering as much anymore.

I sat up to look around. "We're in a tunnel."

All around us was dirt, more dirt, and even more dirt. A few roots peaked through the ceiling and walls, but it was unquestionable, we were surrounded by millions of tons of dirt packed and moved until they formed tunnels. We were in the Puppet Master's tunnel system.

"Really? What was your first clue, Sherlock?"

"Who's Sherlock?" I asked as I looked at her.

She shook her head and waved me off.

Then, her eyes went wide and she pointed behind me. I turned to look and there was a hybrid, sitting up, staring at the two of us.

It tilted its head to the side, then opened its mouth. *He* tried to speak to us, but all that escaped his mouth was chittering and guttural noises that seemed to originate from deep in his throat.

He looked confused, just as much as we were.

I slowly reached down towards my waist where my knife was and he looked down at my hand.

His eyes narrowed, but the noises continued to sound more confused than anything else. As my hand touched the hilt of my knife, he snarled and shook his head.

I took my hand off the knife, barely, and he stopped snarling, returning to the chittering noises he was making.

"This is normal?" I heard Maki ask from behind me.

"I have no idea," I answered. "I've never seen a hybrid act this way, ever. Something's different."

Maki nodded. As he continued to sniff the air, I quietly unhooked my knife. Suddenly, it stood up and went to a wall and started scratching at it.

I knew I should have killed this thing immediately, but I was transfixed by what it was doing and how it was acting.

After a few moments of digging at the wall, a pair of vines were exposed and the hybrid's demeanor changed even more.

He was no longer acting confused or like it was lost, it was now entranced. He reached out and hesitated a bit before touching the vines.

His touch seemed loving. He was caressing the vines.

Maki and I looked at one another, both of us shrugging at the other at our unspoken question.

What was this thing doing? I looked back at it to see it still caressing the vines, and the vines seemed to be moving with the caressing, as if it enjoyed the attention.

I knew the vines belonged to the Puppet Master, so was the Puppet Master enjoying this? Was he responsible for the new possessed beings that acted so much like the Xathi hybrids?

A slight throbbing from my abdomen drew my attention away. I was still bleeding.

I could hear Maki scooting herself close to me.

She looked up at me, and I could see genuine concern in her eyes.

She was worried.

So was I.

While I kept an eye on the hybrid and this awkward love-fest happening with a vine, she took the opportunity to stitch me up.

A small grunt of pain from me brought the hybrid around, the look of rapture on its face changing as it recognized that I was still there.

However, he, it, whatever, did not look at us with anger or malice, but with a sense of pity.

I never wanted my knife in my hand more in my life.

It turned back to look at the vines, then back at us.

Then, he looked down to see Maki finishing off the stitches and the blood covering my clothes. He tilted his head and stared, as if trying to figure out what was going on. As Maki moved away from me, the hybrid looked at her and smiled.

Then, without warning, it let out an ear splitting screech which forced Maki and I to both cover our ears and close our eyes momentarily in pain.

I opened mine back up quickly to see the hybrid take a hesitant step towards us, then he turned and started running down the tunnel.

I shot to my feet and began the chase, Maki yelling at me from behind. "What are you doing?"

I couldn't let the hybrid escape or reach the Puppet Master. I had to stop it before it could cause any harm that we were unable to deal with. He was fast for a short little human, I was barely able to keep up with him.

The only reason I didn't get lost was because I was able to keep him just in sight around every corner. Finally, I rounded another corner and there it was, staring at a creature that engulfed every centimeter of my vision.

A giant plant grew into a humanoid form the size of a very large and tall mountain, with a lush garden in the background. The hybrid stood there, staring at it.

There was a gasp behind me.

It was Maki finally catching up and seeing the Puppet Master for the first time just as I had. He was an imposing being.

To think, he controlled and made the planet live, and here he was, engaged in a staring contest with what used to be a human male.

The hybrid began making guttural noises that seemed to be mixed with speech, but it wasn't a language that I understood, or had ever heard of. I looked back at Maki and she shared the same look on her face that I must have.

She didn't know either.

I was at a loss. What was happening here? Were they communicating? Plotting?

Was the Puppet Master an enemy after all?

I had to stop this. I reached down and drew my knife, then began a slow, quiet approach behind the hybrid.

If the Puppet Master was an enemy, he would let the hybrid know, possibly even defend him.

If the Puppet Master was our friend as he said, then he would let me kill the creature.

I crept as quietly as I could, and just when I was only a couple of paces away, something happened.

The Puppet Master moved.

Not his vines, but his enormous body. He moved

closer to the hybrid, staring at it with a measure of curiosity usually levelled at a science experiment.

Then, without warning, the Puppet Master opened his mouth and let out an animalistic, primal, almost painful roar that shook the earth around us.

I dropped to a knee and saw through my peripheral that Maki was laying on the ground, her arms over her ears as best as she could.

The hybrid started to retreat, a noise coming from it that I recognized as pure and utter fear.

The Puppet Master lurched forward and dozens of vines erupted from the walls. I launched myself at Maki and covered her while chaos reigned behind me.

There were sounds coming from behind us that scared me.

There was ripping and rending and tearing and other noises that I didn't know a body could make when it was being torn apart by a monster the size of a planet.

Maki screamed beneath me as she tried to roll herself deeper into a ball beneath me.

Finally, the noise stopped and the only thing we could hear was our own panicked breathing.

I looked back to see pieces, that was all that was left. Pieces.

I don't believe that we would have ever managed to

put that hybrid back together again, even if we wanted to.

The Puppet Master was staring at me. *"We must speak."*

It took me a moment to realize that what I had heard was his voice, in my head.

"I repeat, we must speak."

Right, then.

After that show of force, I wasn't going to argue.

MAKI

Åll that I could feel was adrenaline.
It was coursing through my veins like a drug, shifting the atmosphere, changing the world around me, leaving me a frantic, excited mess.

I wanted to pinch myself, it seemed such an unlikely occurrence.

Going through the rift, tumbling and contorting to travel from one spot to the next had been weird enough.

But now came this even more surreal moment, one that I couldn't get a handle on because my whole body was trembling. It wasn't fear that I felt however, it was intrigue.

Disregarding Tyehn completely, I dived into a tailspin, my words tumbling out of me like water.

"Holy shit, you're the Puppet Master, *the* Puppet Master. Wow." I managed to briefly pause to take in some more air — I was going to need it — and then dove right back in. "I have questions,"

"Maki, now's not the—" Tyehn tried to explain.

"Shush, I'm busy," I shooed him with my hands, hoping to quiet him so that I could continue. "So, are you an enemy or really a good guy? Are the new hybrid critters your doing? Oooh, what do you eat — *do* you eat? Where do you come from? Do you always speak telepathically or does it depend?"

I couldn't stop myself, the words just poured on and on. There wasn't an off switch for me to press, even if I'd wanted to.

A lot of what I was asking had little meaning in the grand scheme of things, but my mind was on autopilot, unable to stop itself.

I simply moved from one curiosity to the next, leaving poor Tyehn to stare in horrified disbelief.

The Puppet Master however, calmly regarded me. This piqued my curiosity even more because it possessed the power to stop me, to *kill* me.

Yet it waited for me to ride out the last embers of my adrenaline.

It was gracious in how it conducted itself, the decades of its existence having shaped how it saw the world; it was a wise old sage compared to us rambunctious younglings.

"Please, still your mind," Came the most tranquil yet intense voice inside my head.

Immediately I stopped.

It was like falling into a deep trance.

Only unlike the hybrids, I was still my own person, in command of my own senses. Still, the experience was equally as surprising as it was thrilling.

Eager to hear more, I found myself able to stem the torrent of questions building up inside of me, at least for the time being.

Tyehn looked a bit relieved, though I noticed he still appeared tense. I could tell that the gentle giant I knew was still uncertain of where the lines in the sand lay.

"Thank you." It was a thunderous tone, but there was a gentleness to it as well. As organic as the vines trailing from its body, the Puppet Master incited a series of fervent emotions in all who stood before it. *"I understand you have questions, but time is of the essence. We must speak quickly, before others come."*

When I heard the word "others", I instantly felt less excited, my disquiet starting to match Tyehn's.

More hybrids would prove a challenge, even in spite of our combined levels of skill. There'd been one too many hairy moments before now, I didn't relish the thought of more, even if the Puppet Master decided to help.

Appreciating the urgency of the matter, both Tyehn and I remained silent. In truth, it was much easier for Tyehn to keep his mouth shut than it was for me.

Once again, the questions were threatening to overflow, my racing mind desperately in need of an outlet.

Never in my life had I struggled to keep my mouth as still as I did now. It wasn't in my nature to be quiet.

I was born to investigate, my natural love for learning always encouraging me to seek out new discoveries. It had served me well up until this point, and so I wasn't about to turn my back on that natural instinct.

"As you rightly stated, I'm the Puppet Master. My life is intertwined with this very planet: all life flows through me. I'm a beginning and an end to it. If I die, the planet dies with it."

My mouth gaped open as I took in his words. Rumors had always circulated about the Puppet Master, but it was often hard to tell fact from fiction.

All of us were guilty of getting carried away with the idea of this all seeing, all knowing entity — there was a certain romance to it.

One steeped in mystery. It charmed you, drawing you in.

"*Your caution is understandable, but there's a greater threat than I.*"

"The horde." I heard Tyehn mumble, more to himself than to us. In spite of his hushed tone however, his words still rang true. I doubted there was anywhere the Puppet Master's abilities couldn't reach.

"*Yes. These beings may be human, but they're controlled by entities known as the Ancient Enemies. They're non corporeal beings, unable to withstand physical contact, and so they assume control of a host. Humans serve as their host. They are pliable and able to receive suggestions. However, some hosts react differently.*"

I'd heard of some whisperings of people who had changed demeanors.

Everyone had whispered about it. Some people struggled and some people were complete opposites from how they'd acted before.

And then, there was what we'd seen in the jungle.

"*They really are possessed,*" I thought.

"*You're right,*" My eyes grew wide when I heard this. Although it made sense that the Puppet Master could hear our thoughts, it was still unnerving. It was the deepest invasion of privacy, yet it felt light due to the subtlety of his actions. "*I have seen some hosts who could resist their power, while others proved too weak of mind to fight back.*"

There was no comfort in knowing this. What we'd seen had changed us forever.

Even if we could understand the reason for the changes in people we'd known, it didn't make the situation any easier to handle.

How could it?

If the Puppet Master was to be trusted, which it seemed that it could be, then we were dealing with an unknown that had limitless capabilities.

To add to the mounting hurdles that posed, we then had to deal with the susceptibility of humans; millions were at risk.

Looking back on how the hybrid had been obliterated, it made sense for the carnage we'd been forced to witness.

Even if I still didn't appreciate it, my sore throat a reminder of what I'd seen. It had been the most guttural sounding dismemberment I'd ever heard, and its sounds would stay with me forever.

But if these Ancient Enemies were to be as feared as it seemed, it easily explained why the Puppet Master had reacted so violently.

Why it had torn the thing limb from limb, leaving nothing but bloody pieces of brittle bone and crimson liquid.

I shuddered just thinking about it, my eyes quickly looking around at the remains.

Did that fate await me?

Nothing had been said about how likely resistance was, which seemed to suggest that it was rare for a host to fight back.

If that was true, my own mind, body, and soul could be next. It was an idea that didn't bear thinking about. Yet I couldn't prevent the nightmare of its imagery from flashing inside my mind's eye.

I didn't want to end up like that. I *couldn't* end up like that.

Desperate to learn more, I pushed back my dread and tried to focus on what we could do in the present; the future was still a long way off. At least for now.

"Is their purpose simply to take someone over so that they can interact on a physical level?" I felt like a child stumbling in matters I didn't understand, which was plain ridiculous.

I'd spent years researching and immersing myself inside academic study — topics like this were within my comfort zone. In a way.

Nothing could quite prepare you for *this*.

A tendril from the Puppet Master reached out and pawed at the bloody debris before it. There was a tenderness to its touch, even in spite of how it talked about the Ancient Enemies with disdain.

It seemed that there was mutual respect between the two of them, but ultimately, they couldn't easily coexist.

"These possessed beings are created with a specific purpose in mind, one far greater than the need to interact with the physical world."

"What's that then?" I asked exasperatedly.

Although I relished being able to stand before such a foreboding yet strangely beautiful creature, I didn't want to be spoon fed information.

If this was going to be a battle for survival, we needed to be better prepared.

We didn't have time to avoid finding the truth, no matter how harsh it was.

"These beings are here to kill me."

"Oh god," I murmured, the gravity of the situation finally setting in.

Judging by the silence gripping Tyehn, he was as troubled as I. "If the Ancient Enemies control enough humans, they could take over the planet. They'd be unstoppable," he said.

And the worst of all would be that nobody would see it coming.

Mankind would be powerless to stop the transition to subservient puppet because they lacked the strength to do so.

Our own genetic design made us weak.

Some would overthrow the mind control, but not enough.

We'd be swarmed.

These Ancient Enemies would gain complete control.

And this planet would die.

"So, you know them," I said.

I made sure it was phrased as a statement, not a question.

"Yes. I know the Ancient Enemies."

"How?"

"Our peoples have fought a war for countless millions of years," he answered me.

I was absolutely floored. Here was an entity that was who knows how old, capable of creating a planet, supporting life on said planet, and could most likely destroy said planet with little effort, and he had just told me that they've been at war with some non corporeal beings that take over people's minds and can change them into literal mindless beasts.

"I will not apologize for my past associations with

creatures that had come to fool us all. I will, however, apologize for forgetting who they were and what they showed themselves to be many ages ago."

"I forgot you could read minds, as well," I said with a slight smirk after my initial shock of him answering my mental questions.

"I do my best to not do so, friend Tyehn. However, when there are moments such as this where direct conversation is needed, I find it much quicker and far more efficient to do so. It allows me to understand a person's true objectives."

"Okay," I nodded. "I understand that. I do. What was that host's objective?"

"Information. There were two minds fighting, two minds studying, and two minds attempting to understand what they were seeing. The human mind had managed to dominate, but it was a primitive domination led purely by curiosity and a willingness to learn. It was later, when the other mind began to gain control that I was able to understand what was at stake. I fear, however, that I was too late in eliminating the threat before his message was sent."

"What does that mean?"

"The Ancient Enemies, for they are as old as my own kind, perhaps older, and their name forgotten to the ether of the universe, represent conflict and chaos whereas my kind represent growth and harmony. They believe that progress comes from evolution. And that evolution comes from strife.

They seek war to grow. Just as we seek to let life grow without interruption."

"How did they become your 'Ancient Enemies'?" Maki asked from next to me.

Both of us were sitting down at the edge of a drop-off where we were looking down at a beautiful wonderland of plant-life, water, and creatures living under the surface of the planet, and all of it maintained by this creature that was speaking into our heads.

"How long has this been going on?"

"This conflict has replayed itself since the birth of our civilizations. But we are but children in this universe."

"Then, back to Maki's question, how did they become your enemy?" I asked.

"They became more interested in learning how to control the other life, the life that came to us over the life we created. They began to gain control of that life, taking them over so that they would have physical bodies. At first, we did not argue their choices because they took those people and did good things. They built, they created, and they ended conflicts that would have destroyed civilizations that have since brought about so much for the rest of the universe.

"However, they began to become more and more demanding, more and more zealous in their actions. Overzealous in many cases. When they wished to join with us in order to create 'better life' as they felt was needed, we hesitated. What was at first a partnership soon turned into a

*takeover. They began to either enslave the mind of the host,
or simply burned the mind out and took over the body for
themselves. They wanted to do the same with my own
brothers and sisters. That was the beginning of our battles
with them."*

"So, wait," Maki said. "You're telling us that you and
these Ancient Enemies of yours are responsible for life
in the universe?"

*"No. Sentient life has always existed. We are merely
responsible for the homes in which sentient life lives."*

"Damn."

I looked down at Maki to see that she was not
dealing with this information well. I could see her
trying to process the information, and I could only
imagine what she was thinking.

The idea that the Puppet Master and his kind
created worlds for us all to live on, did they create my
home? Did they create the planets of my system? Were
they responsible for the different types of life, plant or
animal, that my people lived with?

Then, to find out that they had a partner that
betrayed their trust.

*"It is difficult to speak of things such as this. Not because
it is painful, but because it has happened so many millennia
ago that even my own memory strains to find all of the
pathways to the past. The Ancient Enemies became ruthless,
more insistent on taking over minds, even wiping out entire*

species in their attempts to take over my kind. We resisted for years that have been lost to time, never to be remembered or regained. We fought one another for so long that time lost meaning."

"How did you manage to defeat them?" I asked.

"I do not remember. I only remember that we finally defeated them and sent them away. Then, my kind spread out throughout the universe, doing our best to escape everything that had happened and to ensure that we would never be caught together. I came here, covered myself and established life here, then fell asleep. My unconscious mind recognizes that you," he indicated with a vine pointing at Maki, *"and the rest of your people were not the first here, as I'm sure you've discovered."*

Maki nodded.

"In truth, I remember seven different sentient species here before your kind, almost all dying out or leaving long before your people came into existence."

My own eyes went wide at hearing that.

How old was this world?

If Puppet Master was millions of centuries old, how old was this world if this is what he made to hide himself and sleep?

"Older than three of her Earths. Older than three of your own home," he answered my silent question. That was interesting information, to find out that my home was as old as Maki's. *"This world, that you have dubbed Ankau,*

is older than both of your worlds. And, I fear that it has been found by the Ancient Enemies that wish to take over."

"How bad is it?"

"The ones that have come through thus far are the weaker ones. They are only capable of taking over the humans that are weaker in mind. Perhaps 'weak' is the inappropriate word. There is something within the human mind that appeals to the Enemy, that allows them a quicker connection. I do not know how they have managed to find me, but they are here and they are using the humans to attempt to establish a hold on this part of reality."

Maki and I looked at one another. What were we supposed to do now?

"How do we fight them?"

"I do not remember."

"Okay. Then we need to get more people together on this. Can you speak to Rouhr and the others about this?" I asked.

"I already have. I've been carrying this same conversation with him as I have with you. It is surprising how similar your reactions and questions have been."

I was mildly flattered at the thought that I shared a similar mentality to the General.

Then, something hit me. "What about my team? Can you reach them? Do you know if they're okay? We were attacked by humans possessed by the Ancient Enemies on the surface."

"I have reached out to them in order to ascertain their well-being. I am happy to tell you that they are all alive and well. As a matter of fact, your commander, Sk'lar, is not only happy that you are safe, but also highly agitated with your disappearance and says 'Tell his ass to get back to base now or he'll be cleaning the latrines for a month.' *I believe he is merely attempting to keep up appearances."*

"Thank you," I said with a smile. It felt good to know that the team was okay. I looked at Maki who was also smiling.

"I'm glad your friends are okay."

"Thank you. I'm sorry all of this is happening."

She shrugged. "Not like you made it happen. Did you?"

I cocked an eyebrow at her question.

"Didn't think so," she said. "What do we do now?"

"I don't know. We need to get back to the others so we can make a plan."

"How do we do that?"

I shrugged and moved my fingers to pantomime walking. She shook her head.

"I will help lead you to the surface and to your team."

"Thank you," Maki and I said in unison.

MAKI

The relief on his face had been wonderful. In the brief time I'd been able to observe them together, I'd recognized the bond between Tyehn and his teammates, however this simply solidified it even more.

I felt privileged being able to witness his joy at learning his team were safe. Tyehn was a soldier, for all intent and purposes, yet the gentle nature behind his strength was what truly defined him. My admiration didn't come cheap, but he'd earned it.

We'd been given a lot of information. Too much, some might say. But for us, me especially, it was the encouragement I needed to power forward; we knew what we were facing now.

There were still missing details, blanks to be filled

in, but we knew the basics. The Ancient Enemies were formidable in spite of their true forms, and they didn't suffer rejection lightly. It was conform or be controlled by force.

Neither option suited me.

I'd die first.

Keeping in step with Tyehn, I looked around the tunnel curiously. "Where does this come out again?" I couldn't help but ask.

He should have been used to it by now, and if he wasn't, it was tough shit.

"Always with the questions," Tyehn chuckled. "It'll bring us to Nyheim. We can regroup with the others there and share what we've learned from the Puppet Master."

"Assuming we don't get attacked again." I quipped.

"I love the optimism you bring, Maki." He looked to the side and winked at me, his eyes twinkling playfully.

Once again, I noticed how pearly his irises were, how the gray had depth even in spite of their lack of color.

They were beautiful. Mesmerizing. I could get lost in them if I looked deeply enough...

"You still with me?" He raised an eyebrow my way.

"Yeah, sorry, in a daze." Then I awkwardly laughed, my trill turning into an awkward snort. "Not like the possessed, obviously."

"Too soon, Maki, too soon." Tyehn rolled his eyes, but I could tell that he wanted to laugh.

Given our recent brush with death, it was good that we could poke fun at nearly dying. It made our struggles seem less frightening and more worthwhile, more badass.

I grinned to myself.

We *were* badass. We couldn't be anything else, we'd met the freakin' Puppet Master!

After our back and forth, we fell into a contented silence, the two of us happy to be in the others' company.

I appreciated being able to do that with someone, it wasn't often I got the chance. Being as brazen as I could be had its drawbacks, chiefly people not liking me. I didn't care most of the time.

However, every now and then, it was refreshing to find someone who took my hard edges with the smoother ones.

As we reached the end and entered the city, I couldn't help but notice how different it was from other smaller towns or even the jungle.

It was chaotic, busy and bustling. Everywhere looked a space was occupied by someone, everybody so consumed with their own lives that they didn't stop to look. To them, this place was just another backdrop.

They'd seen it a dozen times over, it wasn't new to

them anymore. But for me? It was awe inspiring. It didn't matter how many times I saw this place, it would never get old.

"Tyehn!" Before I even turned, I knew it was one of his teammates.

The two rushed to each other and embraced, the joy on both their faces palpable. Then his other teammates came in.

Each of them were glad to see the others were okay, that their trials hadn't been for nothing. They'd made it. I gaily observed them, happy to see how they all banded together like family; they were part of one another.

"We wondered when you'd turn up!" Suddenly another voice came into play.

Turning, I saw two more groups coming towards us, my face dropping in awe as I watched them. They were massive.

Formidable. In seeing them, I could tell that Tyehn wasn't the biggest of the teams. That was a bit shocking.

They were mixed in their species — Valorni, Skotan, Human — there was so much diversity surrounding me.

Having become so used to the hateful ire of anti-alien sentiment, it was heartwarming to be among so many different peoples; this was what it could be like if everyone got along. It was a nice daydream.

Nevertheless, I knew all too well that ignorance

rarely changed. And if it did, it'd merely morph into something uglier over time.

We humans were bastards like that.

I assumed no more surprises were in store, but then I spotted Amira Calder.

Holy shit, it really *was* her.

Everyone knew who she was, and if they didn't, they were an idiot.

Fools. This woman had made one of the biggest discoveries of our time, the temple to the east a treasure of history I was pleased had been found.

I couldn't not say hello.

Pushing past Tyehn while he smiled and chatted with his friends, I barged my way towards her.

Deep brown eyes clocked me before I'd gotten close, yet they didn't hold any reservations. In fact, they softened as I made my approach.

"Hey, wow, um, okay. So, you have no clue who I am, but I had to say hi, I mean, you're Amira, there's no way I couldn't." My cheeks flushed a little then. "I'm talking a lot, aren't I? Yeah, yeah I am."

"I don't think I've met anyone as thrilled to meet me before. I like it." Her grin was small compared to mine, but it wasn't any less genuine.

Few people indulged me, mainly because they didn't know how to. I was this excited ball of energy, hard to handle.

Amira, however, took that in her stride. She remained gracious the entire time, her face always creased into a warm smile.

"I have questions—"

"What she means is that she has *loads* of them, as in you'll be here all day." Tyehn smirked at me as he said this.

He knew me far too well by now, I was being predictable to him.

"Look, questions are necessary, you can't keep quiet on things that make you curious. The world would be so dull if we did that." Then I gave him a sassy wiggle of my head. "If you don't like it, you know where to go."

"Ohhhh, koso." Jalok laughed, the rest of the teams enjoying the banter.

It was nice to be so immersed in their group dynamics, as if I was one of them, as if I belonged.

Before I'd met them, I'd been part of groups before, but none as eclectic as this. Nor had anyone ever understood my humor and its whims as well as Tyehn did.

We worked together well.

Not just running for our lives, and meeting Ancient Enemies, but in the humor we shared.

I wasn't in a rush to tell him this, mind.

Mainly because I didn't want to give him the smug satisfaction in knowing. As I thought on this, I grinned his way, both his eyebrows arching as he tried to guess my meaning.

Ignoring the little jibes being made, I returned my attention to Amira — there was so much to ask her, yet so little time.

Not only was she a name associated with discovery, but being the sister of Jeneva also made her a person of interest.

Being related to the first Skotan/Human baby naturally got people talking about you. And while I didn't want to gossip, I'd be lying if I pretended not to care.

"How's the baby? What's it like? Is Jeneva coping well since becoming a mom or is it tough work?"

Amira stifled her giggles with a hand, leading me to swiftly realize that I was doing it again. I was asking a thousand questions a minute.

I didn't dare look Tyehn's way.

"They're doing well, thank you. Jeneva is a wonderful mom, and Vrehx a good father. As for the baby, he's *different*, but he's wonderfully unique in his own way."

Then Amira shifted our topic to less interesting subjects: me. "What about you, you know so much about me but I know nothing about you."

I was flattered that she wanted to know.

My intention was to keep my personal history light,

nothing too in-depth. However, I soon became blindingly aware of how much I was sharing, or as Tyehn would say, *oversharing.*

Not wishing to bore anyone to death, I allowed my tales to peter out. Besides, I assumed they'd be sticking around for a while yet, so there'd be plenty of time to talk more. Hopefully about things other than myself.

Leaving Amira to integrate back into the main group, I shot Tyehn a sideways smile as he saddled up beside me.

"You just love talking, don't you." He wasn't asking, he was telling.

"Well, if you don't like it, you can always do something about it."

"I intend to." I was about to ask him what the hell he was on about, but before I could he leaned in and planted a kiss on my lips.

My eyes flashed with surprise, then softened into a hazy look of lust as I relaxed into him.

It was the briefest of kisses, more short-lived than I'd have liked.

But when Tyehn pulled away, grinning at me, I was certain it wouldn't be our last.

TYEHN

"Hold still, you big baby."

"Easy for you to say."

The medic grinned as he finished redoing my stitches. Overhead lights cast an ugly yellow luminance over the procedure room.

A few sticky pads had been stuck all over my body, taking my vitals, but except for the gash in my belly I was just fine.

Better than fine.

The memory of Maki's lips against my own lingered in my mind. It made dealing with the pain of the minor surgery much easier to bear.

A knock came at the door.

Due to the hectic couple days I'd had, I jumped and the medic bitched me out for not holding still.

Seconds later Dax came strolling in, still slinging that damn crossbow. I was starting to wonder if it shared a bed with him and his old lady.

"Tyehn, it seems you can't not get hurt."

"Not without disrupting my routine."

"You should pick a different routine. Seriously."

He slapped me on the shoulder, causing the medic to glare at him dangerously.

But Dax was the type who just didn't care.

"How did that molecular sword work out?"

"Now that I had no complaints about. Worked like a charm. I felt like Gonnad the Barbarian with that thing in my hands."

The medic rolled his eyes, but I couldn't figure out why.

Maki had told me that she liked an old Earth holovid about a barbarian named Gonnad.

At least that's what I thought his name was.

Unless... Gonnad was a legendary hero from Earth so maybe I was being blasphemous.

"Well, I'm glad that you made it out in one piece." He stared at the cut on my abdomen. "Or at least mostly in one piece."

"Yeah, you should see the other guy."

I cocked an eyebrow up at Dax and tried to sound as casual as possible.

"So how is Keith doing?"

Dax's face scrunched up and he took a breath before answering.

"Today, he's doing fine—mentally, at least. You banged him up pretty good."

"Today?"

"Yeah, the other day his brain scans came back all weird. But now he's feeling like his old self again. He asked about you. Apparently, he has no memory of what happened after you guys started working out."

"That could be the concussion I gave him, but I don't think so."

Dax arched an eyebrow in query, and I glanced over at the medic.

"If you're all done, can you give us a minute?"

"Sure, you're good to go, big guy. Just take it easy for a few days so you don't bust your stitches."

"I'd like nothing better than to take it easy. Thanks."

The medic strolled out of the room and shut the door.

Once we were alone, I told Dax what the Puppet Master said about the Ancient Enemies.

"Non-corporeal beings? That's a new one on me. How do you fight something you can't see or touch?"

I shrugged, which sent pain shooting through my newly stitched wound.

"I'm sure the scientists are working on it."

"Time was, you were a scientist."

"I still am, really. I just kill on the side."

Dax pursed his lips and leaned against the exam table.

"So, the Ancient Enemies, they can take over anyone?"

"Yeah, though some people seem to be more resistant than others. Jalok's woman's brother apparently could fight it off somewhat, but Keith couldn't."

"Well, we all know Keith is a meathead who smashes first and asks questions never."

We both enjoyed a laugh at that, but soon enough we grew somber again.

"I wonder if maybe some sort of meditation would work." Dax grasped at the air as if trying to pluck at the right words. "You know, some sort of transcendental mental state that would render you immune to their influence?"

"You'd know about that better than me. I'm just a hydrologist with a big gun."

"There has to be some sort of counter measure we can come up with. It's pretty scary that the Ancient Enemies could take over someone at any time."

"Yeah. I was thinking that too." I took a deep breath before I continued. "I mean, what if they took over someone higher up the chain of command and ordered us to open fire on civilians or some srell? We really need some sort of code word to prevent that."

"Unless the Ancient Enemies are privy to the memories of their host."

That notion made us both pretty tight lipped for a while. I poked at my stitches just to see what hurt the most while Dax fiddled with his crossbow.

"Would you like to get out of here?"

"Yes." I rose up from the table, slid my uniform shirt back on, and made sure to pick up the molecular sword.

I'd been carrying it with me even when off duty. Command turns a blind eye to us grunts carrying a melee weapon.

Unless you were a hot head like Jalok.

They don't trust that guy with tweezers when he's off the clock.

The two of us headed into the hallway. A lot of folks were staring at me, and I could guess why. The story of my battle in the jungle had grown to epic proportions, as such things are wont to do.

"That's him," one nurse whispered to another. "That's the guy I was telling you about."

"The one who chopped a hundred possessed into pieces with that sword?"

Dax laughed and elbowed me in the bicep.

"Hear that, buddy? You're famous."

"Yeah, famously hurting and tired. Let's go grab a brew. Or three. Or a dozen."

"Sure thing, but wouldn't you like to see Keith first?"

I brightened up immediately and nodded.

"Yeah, yeah I think I would. Will they let us in?"

"Let them try and stop us." He clapped me on the shoulder. "Besides, who would deny entry to the hero of the Battle of the Jungle?"

"Oh crap, is that what they're calling me?"

"Nah, I just made it up, but it has a nice ring, doesn't it?"

We trudged on up to Keith's room. There was an armed guard standing outside.

The picky little bastard made me hand over my sword but didn't say shit about Daxion's crossbow. Double standards and all that.

The door popped open and there he was, laid up in a hospital bed with his left leg manacled to the frame.

Another guard stood by, watching warily, while a nurse took his vitals.

Keith's face brightened up as soon as we walked in.

"Hey, Tyehn."

"Keith."

I strode over and we clasped hands. His grip was strong, so I guess he was feeling better. He looked at me abashedly.

"Hey, bro, I'm sorry about attacking you. I wasn't in my right mind."

"I know, Keith. You're not the only one to get his body hijacked."

Dax hissed, and elbowed me in the ribs, right next to my stitches.

"Shit. Sorry."

Keith looked between us and seemed confused.

"What's going on?"

"Nothing, it's just some classified stuff we can't discuss with all these civvies around. Rest assured that no one thinks it was your fault, Keith."

"I'm not so worried about that. I'm just glad I didn't hurt you."

"Fuck that, you smashed my nose pretty good and tried to take my head off with a dumbbell."

Keith's face was crossed by such a look of guilt that I regretted my words.

"I'm sorry. That was unkind. I don't blame you. Not one bit."

"Good." We clasped hands again. "Because I'm still gonna catch up to you on the bench press someday."

"Well, I'm not gonna bet against you. Be well."

I clasped my other hand on top of both of ours and squeezed. Then Daxion and I took our leave.

We headed down to the local watering hole and knocked back a few too many.

We talked about a bunch of crap, but didn't speak any more about the Ancient Enemies.

Some things just shouldn't be the subject of drunken converse.

And I had something, or someone else, on my mind.

MAKI

His drunken state didn't surprise me in the slightest.

In fact, I was glad to see him able to unwind; he'd been like a coiled spring for days, ever since we'd gotten back.

Being able to let loose among friends was the best remedy for him.

I felt an intruder interrupting them like this, but I needed to thank Tyehn for all the help he'd given me — without him, I'd be dead.

My name would have been placed on a memorial somewhere, and I'd have become a forgotten footnote.

History wasn't kind to those who didn't hold significant power. And as much as it saddened me to admit, I was just a nerdy chick, not an influential woman.

Turning his eyes to greet me, I noticed how they gleamed with the haze of merriment.

Tyehn wasn't drunk, but he wasn't one hundred percent sober either.

I grinned at him, enjoying seeing him without his sword in hand, able to relax and make merry instead of being buffeted about by combat.

"Heeeeeey, Maki." He slurred slightly. His speech was... interesting... to say the least.

"Hey you. Someone's been having fun, I see?" I turned my grin's beam onto Daxion then back to Tyehn, the two of them as thick as thieves.

"We have for sure, but it's time for me to turn in." Daxion announced.

Raising up out of his chair, he was awkward. His body no longer able to respond to his brain's orders; I had to stop myself from laughing. "You two don't have too much fun now." He joked just before he left.

Blushing wasn't in my nature.

I didn't normally find people's words embarrassing.

But that had caused a blotch of heat to spread across my cheeks, the suggestion laced in between his words hard to ignore.

Not even his heavy, shuffling feet could detract from my reddening cheeks.

"Are you gonna sit or...?" Tyehn rolled his eyes at my indecisiveness. I gave a small shrug than settled down into the seat Daxion had just left.

For a moment, we enjoyed nothing more than the noise of the bar. Listening to the way everyone chatted without a care in the world — and those that *did* care, were too busy sharing those woes to notice the likes of us.

We were just two oddities in among the others.

Granted, we looked odder than most, but that went without saying when you placed a 5'2" woman with a strapping 6'6" Valorni.

It was noticeable in a big way.

Having ordered myself a drink, the warm nectar of it already sliding down my throat, I fixed Tyehn with a meaningful stare. He returned it in kind, though his focus wasn't as steady.

"I need to thank you, no, I *want* to thank you."

"Wait, what did I do?"

"You saved me. If you hadn't stepped in, hadn't protected me, I'd have been brought back in a bodybag. Or, more likely, left to rot back there."

The idea of being left behind was a chilling one, however it was a harsh reality of what happened when tangling with such adamant enemies.

Death was inevitable. So too was an ugly death, unceremoniously forgotten because nobody had the time to bring you back with them.

Tyehn scoffed at this, much to my surprise. It wasn't a malicious sound, however it still caught me off guard; I couldn't grasp what was so amusing. Noting my confusion, he shook his head by way of an apology.

"Sorry, Maki. I'm not laughing at you, I just don't think you need to thank me for anything — I wasn't going to let you die. Besides, you're tougher than you think." He spoke with such humility, it was sickening yet sweet.

Tyehn genuinely didn't understand what I saw in him, how appreciative I was of his actions.

"Oh, shut up, you!" I mockingly slapped his shoulder as I argued back. "you saved me. Literally saved my life. Don't diminish what you did to try and be humble, you ass."

"So now I'm an ass, huh?"

"Sometimes, yeah."

He stared at me stonily, and I him.

Then we burst into fits of laughter, our chests heaving. It was a good sound, a pure sound.

One which expressed a comfort and familiarity between the two of us; we were alike in so many ways.

And because of that, it made me want to introduce more of my life to him.

What I did, who I was when I wasn't scrambling about alongside him and his team.

Glass in hand, I aimed our talks towards our livelihoods. "You were a hydrologist, right? I didn't imagine that, surely." I was beginning to worry that I had. He laughed, only this time there was an edge to it.

"You didn't imagine it, no. Before the Xathi destroyed everything I held dear, that was my life,"

"Oh fuck, I'm so sorry, Tyehn. I shouldn't have asked."

The sense of worry I felt was tenfold. I'd been so insensitive, not giving a second thought to him maybe not wanting to talk about his past.

"Don't be. Maki, I've made peace with that in my own way, so don't ever feel you can't talk to me." Then he cocked an eyebrow. "You're a geoscientist?"

"And hobby archeologist. A woman of all trades, I'm kinda a big deal." I placed my hands on my hips and tossed my non-existent long hair back, a picture of brilliance and beauty.

Both of us chuckled, Tyehn shaking his head in amused dismay as he did so.

"I don't doubt it." He added in between his chortling.

"Don't doubt what?"

"That you're a big deal."

"Is that why you kissed me?" I bluntly asked, not wanting to dance around the issue any longer.

Tyehn smirked at me then, his expression coltish and alive; he looked gorgeous. Sexy. A powerful man with a playful side. He'd piqued my interest even further, and now it was time to explore its depths.

"Maybe it was," He theorized. "Would that be so bad?" His tone oozed sex, drawing me in, making me wanton.

"I don't think so, though we look quite the pair — little and large!" I cackled.

"It seems to work out fine for Zarik and Miri."

I had no idea who he was talking about and couldn't care less.

His eyes were hazy again, only this time it wasn't the alcohol changing their sheen, it was his passion.

His rising passion for *me*.

I didn't doubt for one second that my expression was similar, though if it was, he didn't say. Instead he just grinned at me, the width of his smile intoxicating.

Feeling emboldened by our flirtations, I decided to take a leap forward.

Slow and steady just wasn't my thing. It never had been and it never would be. I liked actions.

Fast paced, working on instinct; I flourished the more I was exposed to it. I stretched my hand out to his, my fingers tracing lines along his own.

Immediately there was a jolt between us. Not enough to physically shake us, but I felt its surge as if it had rocked my whole body.

"Let's get out of here." I finally suggested. Tyehn's grin instantly deepened.

"Whatever for?"

"You know what for, don't play coy."

Moving with increased speed, we left our drinks unfinished and headed to the door.

Our hands were still interlocked, the touches we shared not fervent enough for our liking. I needed more and so did he.

The streets of Nyheim were quiet, thankfully, as were a great many of the empty houses that lined them in certain areas that were being rebuilt as part of the city's sustainability program.

Spotting one nearby, I led Tyehn inside. At the back of my mind I was surprised that nobody else occupied the spot, but that soon gave way to other thoughts, more carnal thoughts.

When he grabbed me by the waist, I didn't care about anyone else but the two of us.

Our kiss was electric.

Earlier we'd been tentative, unsure of the other.

Now however, we knew exactly what the other wanted. It was filthy, it was perverse, it was passion unbridled by the constraints of conservatism.

As we crashed together, our bodies rubbing against our clothed forms, Tyehn began to undress me.

There was haste to his actions, with my hands

quickly following his lead. Although I'd instigated this, he wasn't about to sit by and let me steer.

He wanted to lead. And while I thrived off of being in charge, this was a rare occasion where I was happy to let him assume control.

Freeing me from my clothes, my panties soon followed. Both of us suddenly naked and writhing against one of the room's barren walls. As he pushed me up and lifted my thighs, I followed his desperate touches with my own.

I opened up to him, wet and ready to feel every inch of what he had to offer. There were so many things I wanted to do to him, for him to do to me, however they could all come later. For now, all I wanted was the rigid muscle of his length inside of me. It was all my mind and body could think about, my other capabilities rendered useless.

Locking eyes with one another, he entered me.

I gasped at the change in sensation. He filled me, my body naturally molding to his. Despite his size, there was no resistance, no awkwardness, we simply fit together like two pieces of the same puzzle.

My head swam as we matched the other's pacing, Tyehn's firm hands keeping me in place. He was holding me with such tenderness, yet the way he took me was anything but. There was an insatiable hunger to it. This had been a long time coming.

The deepness of his touch was incomparable to anything else. As he drew back to thrust inside me again, my walls massaging him, the world around us fell away. There was only us.

"We should've done this sooner," I found myself saying, the words escaping from between my lips before I could stop them.

Throwing my arms over his shoulders, I forced him to lay down on the floor, his hard cock still deep inside me. Once there, my knees on either side of his thighs, I started swaying my hips in a sensual rhythm.

"We should've, yes" he finally said. "But I've been wanting to do this since we met." As if to punctuate his words, he placed both his large hands on my ass and slapped it hard enough to make my whole body shake.

I responded by digging my fingernails into his chest, the hard contour of his pectorals making me so damn wet I couldn't even think straight.

I still couldn't wrap my head around the fact that Tyehn wanted me, that he was hard for me, but I was loving every single second of it. To feel his desire throbbing inside me, his whole body burning with desire, was more than what I could've asked for.

"You feel so damn good," I groaned, closing my eyes as I started riding him more fiercely. He responded in kind, thrusting upward with all of his brute force, and I let out a wild scream, one loud enough to be heard for miles.

Any other time and I would've been worried about being caught having crazy sex like this, but right then I couldn't care any less.

What if someone heard me? What if someone saw us? I didn't care. Let the whole world know that I was having the time of my life.

"I could say the same thing, you know?" His voice came at me as if from the other side of the galaxy, his deep voice wrapping itself around my thoughts, and I surrendered to the moment absolutely.

I rode him as he kept on thrusting, our rhythm a matching one, and it didn't take long before I started feeling a vibrant kind of pressure inside me.

My nerve endings felt as if they were on fire, electricity crackling under my skin. All my thoughts were in disarray, all that lust and desire bouncing against the walls of my head like a pinball, and that was when it happened.

Gritting my teeth, I felt the dam starting to break, my body aching for that sweet release. When the explosion finally took place, it was as if my very soul had burned down to ashes. My inner walls became as tight as a vice around Tyehn's cock, but that didn't seem to stop him. Instead, he just started thrusting even harder, fucking me while I was riding a tidal wave of ecstasy.

My moaning turned into full blown screaming then, and it was as if all strength had left my body. I collapsed on top of Tyehn's naked body, my lungs working overtime to get the air in, and my muscles twitched as pleasure kept on whipping at my nerve endings.

"We're not done yet," he whispered into my ear, and I offered no resistance as he pushed me off of him. I was lying down on the floor, but I didn't even care. I merely let Tyehn go down on his knees between my legs, and I arched my back as he started kissing his way from my right knee to my inner thigh.

My body was still reeling from a violent orgasm when he found my clit with the tip of his tongue, and I found desire welling up inside me once more. It's curious. I've never been a prude or a stranger to sex, but my stamina has never been anything of note. It seemed like the problem wasn't with me, though. With Tyehn, I felt like I could keep on going forever.

Raising my legs, I rested them over his shoulders and afforded him a better angle. He seized the chance without a moment's hesitation, pressing his open mouth against my aching pussy, and I did nothing but moan and scream as he used his tongue to unleash hell upon my body.

"You're too good," I breathed out, tugging on his

hair as if I were afraid he'd escape. I felt more words making their way up my throat, but a violent moan rose up to take their place. Pleasure turned into sound then, ecstasy crashing against me like a wave, and I surrendered to the second orgasm of the day.

And still, we weren't done.

Not yet.

"You're holding back," I whispered, looking down at him as he pulled back from me. His chin was glistening from my own fluids, and that made me feel even more wicked and lustful. "I don't want you to hold back. I want you to give me all you got."

At that, his face lit up.

"Remember you asked for it," he grinned. Grabbing me by the waist, he forced me to turn around and then positioned me on all fours. He closed the distance between us in a moment and, grabbing his cock by the root, he angled it down so that the tip was pressed against my drenched pussy.

I closed my eyes as I felt his fingers digging into my flesh, his hold so strong that I could barely move, and I found myself growling with lust as he slid his whole length inside me. This time there was no taking it slow.

He started thrusting as hard as he could right away, his thighs slapping my ass cheeks over and over again, and I let a wicked grin dance on my lips as the sound of flesh on flesh filled the emptiness of the house.

He claimed me like I had never been fucked before, and my heart tightened up at the experience. I knew that sharing my body with him would be unique, but I never thought it'd be this amazing.

In a way, it was almost transcendental.

"Oh, God," I pushed past gritted teeth, my eyes rolling in their orbits as Tyehn thrusted so hard I wouldn't have been surprised to see he had split me in half. My body reacted by instinct, my fluids dripping down my legs, and I exploded once more.

Except this time, I wasn't the only one.

One final thrust and Tyehn exploded inside me, the warmth of his seed filling me up. His cock throbbed violently against my inner walls, but that just added to my own pleasure. It was maddening.

And even after the pleasure started receding, we remained in place, none of us daring to make a move as a blanket of pleasure and absolute bliss enveloped us.

This…

This was perfection.

TYEHN

I didn't sleep a wink the night after my tryst with Maki. As much as I liked the way she looked, with her clothes off she was even more appealing.

The sex was amazing.

And the connection between us was mind blowing because I really liked her. I really, really liked her.

So, I laid there all night, staring at the ceiling with a big smile on my face with the full knowledge I would be on duty in the morning, and not caring in the slightest.

I was already showered and dressed when the alarm went off and headed out the door.

Being early, I decided to take the long way and enjoy a walk on the way to duty.

The walk to the airfield was oddly pleasant. I should

have been worried about the ancient enemies, or maybe dwelling on our nightmarish journey through the jungle, but there was still a spring in my step.

Sk'lar grinned at me when I headed up the ramp. I cocked an eyebrow at him, because Sk'lar was normally a joyless, dour commander.

He clapped me on the shoulder as I passed him on my way into the shuttle.

"How's that gut wound holding up?"

"Fit to fight commander. Fit to fight."

"I see you have your great big gun and even bigger sword."

And that was weird.... But nothing was going to touch my good mood.

"Never leave home without it."

I headed into the shuttle's cabin, my eyes taking a moment to adjust to the relative gloom. After my vision cleared up, I was expecting to see the rest of Team Three. What I didn't expect to find was Maki sitting in my usual spot.

And that explained Sk'lar. He really had to work on his sense of humor.

"Hey." Her voice had a cute little lilt to it, and her eyes were shining. Damn but I wanted to kiss her at the moment, but I wasn't about to do so in front of the guys.

"Hey." I settled my bulk next to hers, and she

snuggled up to my shoulder. Cazak and Navat chuckled derisively, but Jalok grimaced at them.

"Leave him alone, guys. Just wait until it happens to you."

They scoffed, but they left us alone.

"Maki, what are you doing here?" I asked.

"While you were meandering through the fields I took an air transport over."

"But we're being deployed back to Sauma."

"Yeah, as my personal escort. I need to report in back to my lab."

"For real?"

"Indeed. Until this investigation is through, I've received word that I should stay with an armed escort in the event I encounter any more difficulties as some sort of precautionary measure." She frowned. "The EcoBright team was doing something sketchy out there. And I have a feeling that they knew about the Ancient Enemies already. They were strange, even before we knew they were possessed."

We both looked up at Sk'lar, who was standing in the aisle as the shuttle raised into the air. His implants let him keep his balance, the damn show off. "Not only that, but you're being attached to Maki as her escort until further notice. Just try not to let yourself get too...distracted."

Maki blushed, and I stumbled over my affirmative.

The shuttle ride passed by in a flash. Maki and I spoke the entire time, comparing notes about our scientific fields.

There's a lot more overlap than you might figure. Sooner or later damn near every living thing in the galaxy needs water, so my hydrology knowledge applies more often than not.

Maki was a real pleasure, funny and smart and warm all at the same time. Now that we'd slept together, there was less tension between us.

It was easy to relax and talk to her. The rest of the team cut us some slack and left us alone. Jalok, in particular, was magnanimous, which was way out of character for him. I guess he liked the fact that he was no longer the only one on the team with a human girlfriend.

Well, other than Sk'lar himself, but you don't joke with Sk'lar. You try and do your best not to give him an excuse to bust your balls.

The shuttle settled to the ground, and Maki prepared to disembark.

"Hey, big guy, would you walk a gal to her job?"

"I'd be delighted."

We walked from the airfield to her lab, all the while enduring a lot of stares directed our way.

I know that Maki was self conscious about how

weird we look together, with me being nearly two feet and two hundred pounds taller.

"He's my personal bodyguard," Maki told one of the more curious staffers.

I had to laugh at the notion, since we'd both pulled each other's asses out of the fire multiple times in the jungle.

The two of us headed into her building, and I wound up cooling my heels out in the hall while she talked to her boss.

I couldn't hear much of what they were talking about, but I did get the general gist of the beginning of their conversation.

She was explaining what had happened out in the jungle and how she had been called in for debriefings back in Nyheim.

They kept talking about things for a few as I sat outside the office, people giving me looks but generally leaving me alone as they walked by.

Even the ones that fit me with evil, angry, or even 'deadly' stares left me alone.

Then, the conversation inside changed. I wasn't sure why I was able to hear them more, then I saw Maki's shadow pass by the doorway and realized that it was opened a little more than it had been when she first went in.

She had opened it for me to hear.

"We had another resignation," her boss, a short human she had called Dr. Band with affection, said.

"Who?"

"Maura," came the answer. "She just up and quit. I had to chase her down in the parking lot to figure out why?"

"Wait, Maura? Seriously?"

"Yeah."

"Why? What reason did she give?"

"She said something about how alien interaction is messing things up around here and how it's against the human way."

I heard Maki snort. *"Against the human way,"* she repeated. "What kind of bullshit is that?"

"I don't know," her boss responded. I imagined him shrugging as he answered, his face showing just how lost she felt in this entire situation.

I felt just as lost.

Keith had been one of my best friends since arriving on the planet and dealing with everything. He had been one of my closest confidants, someone that I trusted, so when he suddenly turned on me, it was gut-wrenching.

Hearing the pain in Band's voice—was that really her name or her surname—just reminded me of how bad it felt.

"So, did she say anything specific about the

'interactions'?" I heard Maki ask, her voice oozing sarcasm on the final word.

"No. Which makes no sense because she wasn't known to be an alien hater before all of this. No signs of anything, just suddenly walked in, said she quit, and walks out."

That immediately made me think of the Ancient Enemies and the sudden changes in people. If she was yet another person that suddenly changed attitudes and allegiances, then things were still progressing, and we still had no idea how to stop it.

"So, what are we going to do?" Maki said.

"I don't know. I currently have most of Maura's work on hold, *but*, before you get all hot and bothered, I said 'most.' Her experiments that require constant supervision have been reassigned already. And that leads me to what I need you to do. There are several samples in the vault that I need you to take a look at."

"What? No. I'm not a tech."

"I know that, but with Maura gone, we're short handed and I've had to assign some of the techs to dealing with her work. I'm just glad that Maura was so open about her work and kept copious, highly detailed notes about everything."

"Yeah, whatever."

As they continued to discuss things, I let my

thoughts return to my relationship with Maki and how it was progressing.

I smiled at how it got started, running from the possessed, sleeping and hiding in trees, avoiding death. Not the typical way to begin a relationship.

If you paid any attention to so-called 'relationship experts,' a relationship built on heightened adrenaline levels don't generally last long, but I wasn't planning on letting whatever this was with Maki fail.

"Tyehn."

I looked around, trying to figure out who it was that had spoken my name before realizing that what I had heard was in my mind.

"Puppet Master," I said with my own mind.

"We must speak, my friend."

"Are you sure you want to talk to me? Wouldn't speaking with a team leader or General Rouhr be a better choice?"

"I am sorry, my friend. But the information that I must present is meant for you and Maki, not for the others."

"Wait, me and Maki? Why Maki?"

"I wish to tell the two of you together. Please, come speak to me as soon as possible. Go to the park at the end of the street and I will speak to the both of you there." Then, the connection was gone. It was like something in my head just stopped working.

It was extremely disconcerting and a highly

awkward feeling. I shook my head quickly to clear it and stood up. I peeked my head into the office, a small knock on the door to announce myself. "Sorry to interrupt."

"It's okay, we were finishing up anyway," Band responded.

"That's good," I smiled, then looked at Maki. "Someone wants to speak to us, now. Our new friend," I said, hoping that she got the meaning.

I didn't want to say out loud that it was the Puppet Master. If people were weirded out about human-alien interactions, then the Puppet Master was a whole new level of strange.

Her eyes widened a little, then she turned to Band. "Sorry."

Band waved her off and we left.

But towards what, I wasn't sure.

MAKI

"Where are we going?" I asked.

"I told you already," Tyehn replied. "We're going to see the Puppet Master. Weren't you listening?"

"I was. Have you forgotten all of the navigational skills I've taught you?" I teased in response. "We met the Puppet Master north of here. Not east. This road takes us deeper into the city."

"You haven't taught me anything," he laughed. "Unless you count speeding ahead and hoping I keep up teaching."

"I do."

"Ah. Well, in that case, you've taught me a fair amount," he shrugged. "And the Puppet Master chose the location of the meeting."

"He wants to meet in the city? I thought there was some kind of rule about that?"

"Ordinarily, the Puppet Master isn't supposed to surface within a city," he explained, "not after the dome around Nyheim. However, he says he's found a perfect location."

"How convenient."

"Want to know something else that's convenient?"

"No. I like everything confusing and overly complicated," I snorted.

"You phrase that like it's a joke, but I don't think you realize how confusing and complicated you are," he teased.

"I'm not complicated!" I gasped. "I'm an adrenaline junkie who doesn't like bullshit. What's complicated about that?" I playfully swatted at his arm.

"Everything! The only way to keep you content is to make sure you're on the verge of a near-death experience at every moment."

"That doesn't sound complicated to me," I shrugged.

"You're going to send me to an early grave," he groaned.

"That's why you need to make use of all the survival skills I teach you."

"You're an exhausting individual."

"Work on your cardio."

Tyehn tipped his head back and let out a bellowing laugh. Everyone around us stopped to stare at the giant green alien.

For all they knew, he was demonstrating some kind of war cry. I laughed along to make it clear that the Valorni titan wasn't doing anything sketchy.

I didn't follow the anti-alien movement on the news outlets, but I wouldn't be surprised if a faction was hiding out here.

Sauma would be a good place to hide.

"How much time do we have before the Puppet Master's expecting us?" I asked.

"At the rate you walk, we're going to get there early. Why?"

"It's not my fault I have to practically jog to keep up with you," I said. "And, I'm starving. We're about to pass through the market."

"I could always carry you on my back if your little legs can't take it," he teased.

"These little legs can still crack your bones no matter how dense you say they are."

"Go get some food." He rolled his eyes.

"Don't you want anything?" As we entered the marketplace, I gestured to the rows of stands selling every type of food imaginable.

"I'm fine."

I didn't believe him but I shrugged and walked off toward a stall. Tyehn followed with a curious expression on his face.

"You all right?" I asked.

"Just taking in the strange foods," he explained.

"Don't tell me you're a picky eater."

"I prefer to say that I have a refined palate."

"Follow me." I grabbed his hand and led him to a stall with a red and white striped awning. A woman with skin like tree bark who was as wide as she was tall grinned a toothless grin as I approached.

"Haven't seen you around lately," she said.

"Very funny, Mae." I leaned closer to Tyehn. "She's blind as a sunbat. She hasn't seen anyone lately."

"I'm blind. Not deaf." She swatted me with a dried frond. I dodged with a giggle.

"Eight fried dough balls please, Mae." I reached into my pocket and pulled out a single coin. Mae took the coin and bit it to test for authenticity. "Mae, that only works if you have teeth."

"Hush," she scolded me. "I can taste the difference."

"Whatever you say." I lifted my hands in defeat. Whatever Mae tasted, she liked. She took the coin and handed me a bag filled with freshly fried dough.

"I added cinnamon just for you." She winked at me.

"I didn't even know I was coming by today."

"I know you didn't. But Mae knows." She tapped a finger against her temple and gave me a wink. "Come back soon. And bring your handsome friend with you."

"I thought you said she was blind," Tyehn murmured to me.

"Mae knows," the old woman insisted.

"I want to be just like her when I grow up," I said between bites of fried dough. We walked out of the market and deeper into the city.

"Aren't you grown up?"

"Only physically," I shrugged. "Try one." I offered him the bag.

"No, thank you."

"Try one."

"I'm fine."

"Try one."

"Maki!"

"Tyehn! I'm just going to keep bothering you until we get to where we're going. Then I'm going to bother you afterward."

"Fine," he groaned and shoved his hand into the bag. He pushed the fried dough ball into his mouth and chewed viciously. "Happy?"

"What do you think?"

"It's okay, I suppose," he said once he'd swallowed.

"Liar. You loved it."

"Fine. It's delicious."

"Want another?" I shook the bag at him.

He ate three more.

"We're going in here." He turned me off the main path through a wrought-iron archway.

"The park? We're meeting the Puppet Master here?" I asked. "Genius!"

Tyehn and I strolled through the manicured lawns and gardens that could do with some touching up.

Sauma's priorities had been in places other than landscaping since the Xathi invasion.

"What's that?" I muttered more to myself than to Tyehn. I picked up the pace. In the far corner of the park was a cluster of white. As I approached, I realized it was the same snow that coated the Sika Jungle.

"What's this doing here?" I frowned. I wished I had my pack with me. I'd love to test this snow against the jungle snow to see if it's the same.

The snow in the center of the pile began to shift. I took a few steps back, expecting the worst. Tyehn stepped up to stand beside me.

The snow shifted to reveal the bulb of a massive flower. It was tall enough to come up to my shoulder. I looked up at Tyehn to see if he was excited as I was. He grinned down at me and waggled his brows.

Once the bulb broke through the snow, its petals opened one by one. The underside of the petals were a young green, almost white towards the base of the flower. They opened to reveal the richest, most vibrant magenta I'd ever seen.

The petals were shot through with pale pink veins and mottled with deep violet.

"Wow," I gasped. I couldn't think of anything else to say. In the center of the flower was a red beak. It opened and closed a few times, making a clicking sound with each movement.

"*Greetings.*" A voice flew through my head. I jumped back in surprise, much to Tyehn's amusement.

"What the hell?" I sputtered.

"Hello, Puppet Master," Tyehn said to the beak. "What's so important?"

"Wait up," I said slowly. "I'm loving this new look." Before I could stop myself, I lifted my hands and gave the bulb the finger guns.

"What in the seven suns was that?" Tyehn snorted.

"Don't judge me. I'm trying to make a good impression."

"Oh, I'm judging you."

"*You are wondering why I called you here.*" The Puppet Master declared in my brain. "*I have spent some time meditating on my past and the collective history of our species. I believe I've unlocked a memory, for lack of a better word, in regards to the Ancient Enemies.*"

The smile vanished from my face.

"Tell us everything you remembered," Tyehn urged.

I will try to explain in a way that will make sense to your kind. The Puppet Master's vibrant petals moved slightly as he spoke through our thoughts.

The Ancient Enemies have no corporeal form, at least not one that I can recall. They are like a virus of the consciousness. These memories are painful for me to recount.

"Take your time," I said softly. I reached out and touched the edge of a petal. Beneath my hand, I felt the Puppet Master relax.

They attack the mind and drive it to the point of madness.

"What is the first sign that the Ancient Enemies have targeted a planet?" Tyehn asked.

If they are present, they will immediately look for lifeforms to host them, the Puppet Master explained. *If they are a virus, they need carriers.*

Tyehn and I exchanged a glance. A chill crept down my spine as I thought of the possessed in the jungle.

"Thank you for your information. It will be valuable to us," Tyehn nodded.

I am glad to be of assistance. I will alert you if I remember anything else. The Puppet Master started to fold up its petals but Tyehn stopped it.

"I have one more question," he said. "Why did you request a meeting with us, specifically? Why not General Rouhr or the Mayor of Nyheim?"

The Puppet Master unfolded a petal and rested it on top of my hand.

"Because of her."

TYEHN

I turned an incredulous gaze toward Maki, and reflexively took a step away from her.

"What is the Puppet Master talking about? What makes you so special?"

"I don't know." Maki shook her head in confusion. "I really don't. There's nothing special about me at all."

"I disagree." I flashed her a smile, which she weakly returned.

We turned back to the bizarre talking flower and addressed it, as silly as it seemed.

"Puppet Master, what do you mean by that? Why tell Maki instead of our leaders?"

"Maki was once a host for the Xathi virus, which turned her into a crystalline hybrid. However, unlike anyone else

from the sapient immigrant species, her auto immune response was able to hold off the virus."

I gaped at Maki, unable to comprehend what I was hearing. Maki had been infected by the Xathi?

And turned into a hybrid?

I wasn't sure how I felt about all of that, other than being quite uneasy.

"Maki, is this true?"

Maki sighed, and rubbed the bridge of her nose.

"It's true. I don't know why, no one really does, but for some reason I never fully transformed into a hybrid. When they gave me Mariella and Evie's serum, I responded immediately."

My heart pounded in my chest, and my head ached. From the tension in Maki's shoulders, she was feeling pretty stressed out as well.

As if I hadn't enough to worry about with sorting out my feelings for Maki, the new information dropped into my lap like a ton of bricks.

Maki had been a hybrid, infected, like the creatures which had hounded us relentlessly through the Sauma jungles.

Then it occurred to me that, without the Ancient Enemies creating their own hybrids, Maki and I would likely have never met.

I'm not one for existential angst, but that thought bothered me a great deal.

I addressed the weird flower mouth thing once more.

"So Maki is resistant to the Xathi hybrid virus. So what? The Xathi are old news. We kicked their asses."

That was an exaggeration. In truth we'd barely managed to defeat them with a combination of luck, guile, and determination.

"It's difficult to put into terms your species can understand. But I will try."

"Please do." Maki crossed her legs and sat down on a nearby stone jutting up from the snow covered field.

"It is possible that Maki can resist the Ancient Enemies. Perhaps even defeat them."

Maki and I exchanged worried glances.

"But how?"

"Unknown at this time."

"Great. Just great. So, you call us here to tell us you don't know a damn thing."

Maki gaped at me and put a restraining hand on my forearm. "Tyehn, take it easy."

"Tyehn's apprehension is understandable. I take no offense."

"Good, because Tyehn's big mouth tends to talk without thinking."

Maki grinned at me, perhaps to show that she was kidding.

But suddenly I wasn't so comfortable around her

any more. I kept seeing an image of her with crystalline skin in my mind.

Hybrids might just be my worst nightmare.

Maybe there'd been some sort of mistake.

Perhaps the virus was dormant in her system. My scientific knowledge worked against me, filling my head with wild scenarios where Maki turned into a savage, feral creature bent only on destruction.

Just like the Valorni mother during the Xathi invasion of my home world.

"So, what is it you want us to do?" Maki stood and stepped closer to the flower mouth, hands out as if in supplication. "I assume you need something from me, or you wouldn't have summoned us here."

"Maki is correct. I would like her to work closely with me, as well as your own men and women of science. Perhaps your resistance to the Ancient Enemies can be exploited to help others, or even provide a means of attacking them."

I shook my head and stepped up before the flower's mass.

"Whoa, wait a minute. Are you saying you want to, to what, weaponize Maki? Are you sure that's safe? How can you be certain that it would even work in the first place?"

"Tyehn, calm down."

"I can't calm down. It wasn't so long ago that the

Puppet Master was trying to kill us, and now it wants me to just hand you over to it? Based on a hunch?"

The flower's 'face' adjusted to face more toward me.

"*Your apprehension is understandable. I do not as of yet know exactly how Maki might be of use, only that it is in the realm of possibility. The Ancient Enemies destroyed my—I suppose in your terms it would be my 'people.' I am all that remains. If there is a possibility that they can be defeated once and for all, we must grasp the opportunity. Far more lives than just Maki's are at stake.*"

What the Puppet Master left unsaid was that its own life was probably worth more than Maki's. After all, it was an ancient being, living through countless eons and with a life span that beggared the imagination.

And it was the last of its kind.

But I couldn't help being selfish.

Maybe at that moment I had no idea how I really felt about Maki, but I damn sure didn't want her sacrificed so a giant plant could continue to exist.

Later I realized I was being truly selfish, and a fool as well, because if the Puppet Master died then the planet would die with it.

At the time, however, all I knew was that I didn't trust the Puppet Master.

I also wasn't sure I could trust Maki, either.

"No, Puppet Master." I crossed my arms over my

substantial chest and stuck out my lower lip. "You don't just get to experiment on our people to satisfy a whim or verify a hunch. Our lives have meaning too, you know, even if we're only going to be around for an eyeblink compared to yourself. Maybe that even makes our time more valuable than yours, given that we have so little of it."

"Tyehn, it's okay." Maki turned to the flower mouth. "Puppet Master, I would be more than happy to help you in any way that I can."

"More than happy?" I shook my head in disbelief. My hand snagged onto her bicep and I turned Maki to face me. "More than happy? Is that a human expression? Because it sounds like a dangerous mental condition to me. How can you be more than happy? How can you be even considering this, this monster's ideas at all?"

"The Puppet Master is not a monster." She attempted to jerk her arm out of my grasp, but I didn't release her.

Maki grimaced up at me. "You're hurting me."

I immediately released Maki, fuming mad.

"You know that he has different priorities than we do. There's no telling what his game is. Look, I caught a glimpse into this thing's mind, and I'm still not quite sure I retained my sanity. You can't judge it by human standards. For all we know, it's making up this bullshit about the ancient enemies and is just looking to add you to its collection."

Maki glared up at me, so fiercely I averted my gaze. "You're letting your fear do your talking for you. Why are you acting like such an ass about this? You're not my commander or my owner. I do what I please."

I opened my mouth to respond, but then closed it. Something told me that I was on thin ice and should remain silent until she wound down.

"And don't you dare accuse the Puppet Master of making up stories. If it wanted us dead, we'd be dead. All of us. There's no way for us to fight against the flora and fauna of this world if it all rose against us at once." She rested her hand on my arm. "You're not thinking, Tyehn. You're a man of science. Puzzle it out. If the Puppet Master were truly intent on being our enemy, then why would he make up a story—and an impossible to prove story, at that—about incorporeal beings?"

I realized she was right and heaved a heavy sigh. "Okay, you're right. I'm not thinking things through. It's just, it's just there's a lot going on now, all right? A lot to absorb."

"Hmph." Maki turned back to the Puppet Master's mouthpiece. "What do you want me to do?"

"You must allow me into your mind, so I can interface with you directly."

"All right. I'll do what you need to."

I had little choice but let her.

Maki used to be a hybrid.

How could I ever fully trust her again?

And what did this mean for our new relationship?

MAKI

"You don't have to do this," Tyehn blurted. He had a strange look on his face that I couldn't place. He looked pained, confused, but there was something else in there too.

"I know." My voice trembled when I spoke. "But if there's something in my head that can help us, I want to do it."

"You can change your mind at any time," Tyehn said.

"I'll be fine." I tried to give him a reassuring smile but it looked more like a grimace. "Remember, I'm tougher than you are."

Tyehn choked out a laugh but the worry never left his eyes.

I settled myself in the snow pile beside the Puppet Master.

"Your companion is correct," the Puppet Master said. *"I did not intend to do this today. If you are not comfortable, we can do this another time."*

"No," I snapped. "I'm here. I'm ready. I want to do this now. Putting it off will just make things worse."

"Very well," the Puppet Master said gently.

"I'll be right here the whole time," Tyehn assured me. "I've also signalled on my comm and soon we'll have soldiers stationed at every entrance of the park. No one will disturb you."

"Thank you." I wanted to say more but the words dried up in my mouth. "What's going to happen?"

"I am going to enter your mind," the Puppet Master explained. *"Once I do, we'll be able to access your deepest memories together."*

"You'll be with me?"

"You will be reliving memories in which I am not present. You will not see me but I will be there all the same. If I feel that your distress is too great to the point of causing damage, I will pull you out."

"Okay." I nodded.

"What kind of damage?" Tyehn spoke up.

"The memories we will be accessing may be incredibly painful and scarring. I will not allow Maki to suffer any lasting psychological damage. You have my word."

"It's fine, Tyehn," I assured him. "I'll be fine." I wasn't convinced but hopefully, I could convince him.

"All right," he nodded.

I turned to look at the Puppet Master's vibrant petals.

"Will it hurt?" I asked.

"*You should not feel any pain. If you do, I will pull you out. However, your memories may trick you into thinking you're in real pain rather than remembered pain. Just remember that it's not real. You'll be able to fight through it and keep exploring your memories.*"

"Got it." I gave a jerky nod. "Let's do this."

"I'll be right here," Tyehn repeats in a softer voice.

"I know." This time, my smile looked real.

A vine burst through the snow. It looked like any other vine one would find in the forest, except for it was shot through with pulsing veins of light.

"*This won't hurt,*" the Puppet Master assured me once more.

"I'm ready." I trembled with impatience. "Do it."

The vine wrapped around my arm from my wrist up to my shoulder. The tip of the vine rested against my neck and stretched up to my temple.

I looked up at Tyehn to give him one last smile but I was suddenly pulled into darkness.

I felt myself slipping away.

I tried to keep a firm hold on my mind so that I could analyze what happened around me but it wasn't working.

Something else entered my mind. My whole body recoiled at the feeling I hoped to never feel again.

The Xathi sub-queen I served under merged her consciousness with mine.

I thrashed against it, against her.

Shh, dear creature. A woman's soothing voice washed over my consciousness. **You have no need to fight. I shall protect you.**

My body relaxed. I felt like I was floating on a cloud. My mind still struggled for control. I couldn't give up.

Not again.

Such strength! The voice marveled. **You will make a fine soldier. Let me lead you. I can protect you.**

I don't need protection. I'm strong enough to fight on my own.

A face took shape in my mind's eye.

At first, it was horrible. A transparent, crystalline head with too many eyes and sharp pincers. I recoiled, struggling harder against the grip on my mind.

The true face of the Xathi sub-queen morphed into something else.

The face of a beautiful maiden with skin like milk and hair like corn silk filled my head. Her massive blue eyes sparkled with laughter. Her red lips were parted in a grin.

What do you have to be frightened of? Look at me! I won't hurt you. I want to save you.

That didn't sound so bad. Everything around me crumbled more by the day.

Soon there would be nothing left. I should let her save me while I could still be saved.

That's right, she encouraged. **Let me save you.**

More of my mind slipped away from me.

The Xathi sub-queen traced out a path in my mind. She showed me exactly what to do so that I would be safe.

I could join my friends.

They'd already joined the ranks of the Xathi sub-queen. They were saved. I could be with them again.

I wanted that.

All I had to do was follow a few tiny, simple orders.

I ask for so little and offer you so much, the beautiful Xathi sub-queen hummed to me.

She showed me the horrible monsters that were trying to kill her children and followers.

Towering creatures with green skin and purple bands, red monsters with scales, and grey beings that were half creature, half machine.

They looked familiar. I couldn't quite place the memory.

They must be destroyed. Help me and I will save you, the Xathi sub-queen whispered.

I don't want to fight those creatures.

The Xathi sun-queen expected me to feel fear.

When I didn't, she dove deeper into my mind. She tried to force me to hand over my willpower to her.

I jerked back instinctively. It didn't feel right.

The image of the fair maiden flickered away. The true face of the Xathi sub-Queen showed through her illusion.

No, I didn't want this. I never wanted it. I never will want it.

"Let me go." My voice was weak.

I just want to save you. Why don't you let me save you?

"You don't want to save me." My voice grew stronger with each word. I pushed against the hold of the Xathi sub-queen.

She thrashed in my mind, desperate to dig her claws into me.

"Get out!" I screamed. I kept screaming until my voice was raw and my head felt like it was going to explode.

Suddenly, the Xathi sub-queen vanished.

I looked around. I was in a clearing in the forest. All around me were other people fighting against the hold of the Xathi sub-queen.

But they were losing. The person nearest to me turned to face me. Their eyes didn't look right. They snarled and snapped.

When they lunged, I took off into the forest.

I was still in control of my body and my mind but something didn't feel right.

Even though the Xathi sub-queen couldn't hold her grasp on me, she left her mark. When I tried to remember my name, I couldn't.

I had no idea who I was or where I needed to go.

Panic gripped me. My throat closed up as tears welled in my eyes. Maybe I should've let the Xathi sub-queen have me. I needed saving.

"No." I gritted my teeth and pressed onward. There was something I could do. There was always something.

I wandered into a city that I couldn't remember the name of.

Guards that looked like me and guards that looked like the creatures the Xathi sun-queen tried to scare me into fighting approached me.

"Do you think she's one of them?" One asked.

"She's not displaying any of the key symptoms. Her eyes look fine. There are no patches on her. She's not aggressive. Still, let's get her to the clinic. The doc will want to examine her. We can't take any chances."

A red giant with scales took me by my right arm. Someone who looked like me took my left.

"Are you going to save me?" I croaked.

"You've saved yourself," the one on my left said. "We're just going to help you with the last step."

"Oh."

I was taken to a run-down building that looked far nicer on the inside. A smiling woman took me into a room.

She sat me down and poked me with needles. She talked to me, but I couldn't hold the words in my head. She didn't seem bothered that I didn't answer her.

"I'm glad you came in. There's a seed of Xathi corruption within you. You must've worked so hard to fight it off. Don't worry. We'll get rid of it."

Corruption inside me? My insides twisted at the thought.

The woman injected something into me and instructed me to lie down.

"This might be rough," she warned me. "Just lay still and know that it'll pass. You'll feel much better when it does."

At first, it was terrible. Nausea ripped through me. My skull felt like it was going to split open. Chills tore through me. My teeth chattered so violently I worried I would bite off my tongue.

Then it stopped.

Everything I was before the Xathi sub-queen tried to steal my mind came rushing back to me.

My name was Mika Hotaru.

I was a scientist. I loved to climb and explore everything I could find.

I was my own person.

I saved myself.

THE PUPPET MASTER slowly broke the connection to my mind. My memories faded back to blackness.

When I opened my eyes, I was lying on my back in the snow under one of the Puppet Master's stunning petals.

"Mika?" Tyehn called softly.

"She may not be able to speak right away. Her memories were violent. She might need time to recover."

"No," I said. "I'm okay. I'm back."

With the help of Tyehn and the Puppet Master, I sat up.

"What happened? Did you find what you needed to find?"

"I'm not sure," I said. I looked at the Puppet Master.

"It was a good start," the Puppet Master said. *"I've confirmed that you were, in fact, able to fight off the control of the Xathi without outside assistance."*

"That's good, right?" I looked to Tyehn, who nodded. "How did I do that when no one else could?"

"That's an answer I do not yet have," the Puppet Master

replied. *"The important thing is that we know it's possible. Should the Ancient Enemies come for you, you will be able to fight against them."*

TYEHN

The city of Sauma was a beautiful place.

The people that called the city home had incorporated their city into the surrounding jungle, only clearing out what needed to be moved for roads, buildings, and a few parks, and even then, most of those trees were transplanted into different parts of the jungle.

Looking back at original satellite images, I was able to see that the jungle actually expanded several hundred yards in two directions thanks to the transplanted trees.

Add in the falling snow, and the place seemed nearly mystical in nature.

It could almost be a place I could call home.

If it wasn't for the fact that one of the reasons I

might be interested in calling it home, was nearly turned into a Xathi hybrid.

I knew that she wasn't that anymore, but there was still something about that part of her past that bothered me.

I wasn't sure if I could trust her motivations, her thinking.

I was confused by her.

I was confused by my feelings for her, by my assessment of her. She was tough. She was a fighter, a survivor, an intelligent woman with tremendous skills and abilities. She had shown me absolutely nothing to have lost or questioned my trust in her.

It was me.

I had lost faith in who she was because of what the Puppet Master had told me.

The instant he had said that she had been infected by the Xathi, I became unsure of who or what she was.

Something about her had changed in my mind, and no matter how hard I tried to tell myself that she was cured and there was nothing wrong with her anymore, I couldn't shake the feeling that there was something hidden deep inside her that would one day come out and change who I had come to know.

I was standing in an airfield on the edge of the city waiting for Dax to arrive for a pickup. Standing thirty yards to my right were nine crates, each of them filled with food, medicine, and equipment needed to help new civilizations grow and to help combat the anti-alien factions that were still looking for ways to get rid of us.

I only had to wait a few minutes before his shuttle appeared on the horizon.

"This is shuttle Beta-three-seven, coming in. Am I clear for landing?"

I clicked on my comm. "You're all clear Beta-three-seven. Good to hear your voice Dax."

"You too, Tyehn. What's the load?"

"Nine crates, just short of two-thousand pounds."

"Damn, nice supplies. I'm coming down."

I watched as he brought the shuttle to the airfield and brought it to a hover just a few hundred feet above the ground. Retro rockets came on and began to bring it down slowly. In less than thirty seconds, he had it landed on the ground.

As I began my approach, the shuttle bay doors opened and there stood Dax, a man that, even though we were similar in size, he made me feel small. And it wasn't that he was vicious or intimidating, quite the opposite.

He was a good man that abhorred violence.

However, he was exceedingly talented at violence, and his mini-rail gun was enough to even the odds in any fight.

"My friend," I greeted him with a handshake and hug.

"Brother," he said in return. "Whoa. Didn't expect those crates to be so large." I looked back at the crates. I hadn't thought it odd that four of the crates were larger than me while the other five were only slightly smaller.

"Think you got enough room?" I asked with a grin.

"Depends on who's packing," he smiled back. "How are you, my friend?"

"I've been better, if I was being honest."

"And if you weren't being honest?"

"Then I'm doing great."

"Good to hear," he said as we made it to the crates. "Okay, crates one and three go in first on the right hand side, my right. Then bring in the smaller ones and finish off with two and four on the left to offset the weight imbalance," he directed the loading crew.

As they started getting their gear together to load the shuttle, he turned to me. "Come on, let's talk. I don't have to be back at base until sundown, and it's barely breakfast time."

He had a point. The early morning sun shone on the snow, and I myself was feeling a bit hungry.

We made a quick trip on a small hover bike to a nearby cantina that was just opening. They seemed a bit intimidated by two massively sized men coming in as they opened their doors, but they were cordial and polite as they showed us to a table.

We ordered our breakfast and sat back as we waited.

"Talk to me," Dax said as he sipped from his morning coffee.

"Do I have to?"

He sipped at his coffee, and shrugged. "No, but then I won't let you train on my new toys."

"Okay. Fine. It's about something that the Puppet Master told me." I looked away and stared out the window of the cantina. "He told me that Maki used to be a hybrid."

"Say what now?"

"Maki used to be a hybrid. She apparently was able to fight them off before she was fully converted. She managed to get some of Evie's serum to help her get the rest of the way back to normal."

"Okay then. She's normal. What's the deal? What, you like her or something?"

I was unable to answer as our food was delivered. I had come to enjoy steak and eggs with hash browns and bacon.

I noticed that Dax had gone with some sort of meat covered in breading, a brown colored gravy, and chopped potatoes with onions and bell peppers.

"Luurizi fried steak with gravy and potatoes. I love

this stuff," he murmured as he grabbed his utensils and began cutting into his meal.

I grabbed a bottle of some steak sauce that had a bit of a tart taste to it, and poured it on my steak.

"Breakfast. Love what these people come up with for it," I said in awe.

"Same here. Now, answer my question," he said over a bite of food.

I chewed down my bite of steak and proceeded to do just that. "Well, yeah. She's different. She's fearless in ways I never anticipated a human to be. I just, I don't know anymore."

"Let me guess. You're wondering if something is still buried deep inside her that will turn her against you and the rest of us. Am I close?"

I nodded as I put another bite of steak in my mouth.

He shook his head. "You're an idiot."

"Excuse me?"

"Have you not heard of Sylor and Evie? Have you not heard of her fight against one of the Xathi queen?"

"Of course, I have," I answered. "What about it?"

He shook his head in exasperation. He pushed his plate to the side and leaned forward onto the table. "Think it through, dumbass. She was invaded by one of the Xathi queens. She had the queen in her head. Yet, she fought her off and we all trust her because we all know that she's strong and that she defeated the queen. What makes you think that Maki is any weaker?"

I stopped, my fork stopped just shy of my open mouth as my brain absorbed what he had just said. Maki had defeated the Xathi control, just as Evie had. And I trusted Evie with my life.

So, why was I questioning Maki's abilities?

Dax started chuckling. "Now you get it, don't you?"

I looked up at him, chewing on his food as he gave me the 'you're a moron' look. "I hate you," I mumbled as I put my fork in my mouth and bit down on the amazing steak that I had ordered.

"No, you don't. You love me, and you know it."

"Ha, ha. Come on, the eggs are getting cold. We better eat," I said.

He nodded. While we ate, I thought about what he had said. He was right. If I could trust Evie, then I could trust Maki. I had to find her. I had to apologize to her and make things right. I felt bad for what I had done, and I was determined to fix it.

After breakfast, we returned to the shuttle and finished supervising the loading of the crates. "It's been good seeing you, Tyehn. Don't be an idiot with Maki. Guaranteed you won't find someone like her again."

I nodded. "Thank you. I appreciate you helping me pull my head out."

"I was wondering what that popping sound was," he

laughed as we struck fists. I stepped back and watched the door close. I turned and walked away, getting out of the path of the shuttle as it began it's flight sequence. As Dax left, I waved a good-bye and turned back towards the city.

It was time to apologize to Maki.

MAKI

Revelations always troubled me. Sometimes they could be for the better, but most times they knocked you on your ass, leaving you confused and afraid.

This was one of those times.

I was savoring being able to commune with the Puppet Master again, and our latest meeting was no different.

However, it'd been a tiring one, overwhelming in what I'd learned and what we hoped to achieve moving forward.

I wanted to be able to give the Puppet Master more details about when the Xathi had infected me, but I didn't know where to start.

The memories were there, we both knew that much.

However, I wasn't able to tap into them as easily as I'd have liked: my mind was blocking the trauma.

I wasn't sure if this was a byproduct of what I'd gone through, or a safety mechanism my own body had created. Either way, it was screwing me over right now.

The shock of reliving my hybrid past was still tangible. If I thought about it too long, it burned at the back of my eyes, threatening angry tears and self-doubt.

When I'd first seen the humans the Ancient Enemies had possessed, I'd been scared that I could fall prey just as other humans had.

It was bitter-sweet knowing that I couldn't. All of me should have been glad by this, but in learning my past, I'd lost part of my present.

Tyehn had turned on me.

Ever since the Puppet Master's words, he'd been a royal jerk. He'd quickly distanced himself, so much so that our tryst from the previous night before seemed nothing but fantasy.

Worlds I'd dreamed up... All those times where he'd softly kissed me, how I'd led him to that empty house and he'd pinned me against the wall... It suddenly became a part of the past that he wanted to forget.

Tyehn wanted them to be fantasies, for them to be a distant memory until he figured out what he was feeling.

They weren't any of those things, though. They'd been real. But he was determined to undo all that we'd become thus far.

Tyehn had snatched it away from me because he was too blind to see that people could change, that I *had* changed. I hadn't even been aware of the infection taking place, my mind obviously numb to what had happened. It was fine when Keith had behaved that way, but me? I was scorned for it.

Shunned by no one else except for him. I was that troublesome woman he'd foolish had sex with, believing her to be a safe bet when she wasn't.

Normally I'd fight tooth and nail for the truth, however I didn't have the energy anymore.

If he wanted to be a jerk, he could do it on his own time.

Without me. I wouldn't succumb to his subconscious suspicions.

Fuck him.

Cradling a cup of jasmine tea, I moved further into my room, trying to sweep away the niggling doubts my head now harbored.

It had been easy enough to requisition an unoccupied house in town for while I was here.

The problem of staying here by myself though, was that I was haunted by thoughts of Tyehn.

They just wouldn't leave me!

If I thought of Tyehn, I got angry. Then I got angry at myself for not knowing what I once was. Lastly, it all gave way to vexation and despair, leaving me more frustrated than when I started. There was never any peace.

A swift set of knocks on the door alerted me.

Settling my cup down, I moved to answer it.

As I opened the door to see Tyehn's apologetic face, I already knew I wasn't in the mood to deal with him.

His apologies didn't interest me, not anymore. Still, I moved aside to let him in.

"Maki, I, I don't know where to begin — I'm sorry," He looked as genuinely ashamed as his speech sounded, however it all felt a little too late for me. I couldn't forget how he'd been. The image was burned into my retinas.

All those looks I'd given him, seeking his comfort, only to be rejected from afar — he was asking me to forget a lot. I didn't know if I had it in me to overlook his mistakes so quickly. When I'd been a hybrid, I hadn't been in control.

While he'd acted the ass, he'd been fully aware of what he was doing.

"You're sorry, really? Well, if that's all you've got, you can get the hell out." I was venomous as I bit back.

"Please don't be like that." He began, his eyes wide. "How would you have reacted?"

"I wouldn't have turned into this unfeeling, cold-hearted jerk like you have! It was bad enough learning about my past that way, but for you to just drop me, that stung the worst of all." I was fired up now, unstoppable and ready to unleash my fury. "We'd been seeing each other, growing closer, and that new information was enough to paint me untrustworthy?!"

Tyehn sighed.

It was heavy, defeated, almost as if he couldn't handle the guilt he felt. I didn't care. I didn't want to know. He deserved to feel guilty for what he'd put me through. I wasn't upset enough to cry, those moments had long past — I was now just angry.

"Maki,"

"Don't Maki me. *You* abandoned me the moment you thought I was dangerous, conveniently forgetting all the times we'd spent together. You were an asshole."

"Reck, I know." Exasperation forced him to reach out to me; I reacted instantly.

Flying into a rage, I punched with all my might at his chest.

My knuckles rebounded off of his firm muscles, yet still I persisted. One hit turned into two more, and then a torrent of them came. I was raining down my fists on him again and again… yet he never moved.

Never tried to stay my hand.

Flustered, I stopped. I was embarrassing myself by

acting out like this, he was just being diplomatic by humoring me. That was worse than him asking me to stop.

"I'm sorry, I shouldn't have... I'm just... I'm sorry." My words felt hollow and untrue, however the meaning behind them was real. I genuinely didn't mean to behave like a child.

"It's okay," Tyehn replied. My eyes narrowed as I regarded him once more. "I treated you badly, I deserve all I get. You're tired of me, bored of the man I am—"

"Oh, hell no. Don't put that shit on me, not only is it patronizing but it's not true." He wasn't going to play the victim, not on my watch.

"I know it is." Came his feeble response. And that was when I saw red.

I went to slap him, my hand reeling back to land a full blow. However, before I got a hit, he caught my arm mid-air, asking me, calmly, to stop hitting him.

When I yanked free and rounded for a second swing, he lifted me up and folded me into his arms. His voice had lost its calmness now, the annoyance in him growing.

"Stop hitting me, Maki." He growled.

My arms were sandwiched by my sides, rendering me useless, so I opted for a new weapon. Rearing my head back, I slammed my forehead into his with tremendous force. The two of us immediately recoiled from the other.

Naturally, he released me, my body slumping to the floor. Seizing an opportunity to strike another damaging blow, I brought my legs around in a fluid motion, executing a clean leg sweep. As he tumbled down, I was ready.

I moved onto him, climbing on top so that I could be crowned the victor. Tyehn wasn't content to let me win though, his arms grabbing me so that I rolled onto my back as he switched our roles.

Instinctively, my hands flew up to beat at his chest again. I'd take any way possible to hurt him, to land as many blows as possible but he overpowered me.

Before I'd landed my third hit, he pinned my hands above my head. My chest heaving wildly, my lips parted in a twisted grimace, I glared at him. He returned my stare, his eyes burning into mine.

For a few seconds we were locked in a soundless battle of wills, our bodies too exhausted to move.

Then he kissed me.

At first, I fell into it just as I'd done the other times. Then my mind screamed at me that this man a bastard, that he'd done me wrong.

I pulled away, but his lips came crashing back to mine. And while I wanted him to pay, I also wanted to feel the weight of him on me, pushing me down, taking what was his.

The next time I tried to turn away, he handled me with more force. My body responded in kind. My kisses became fervent, crazed even. All I could think about was tearing his clothes off and him screwing me right here, right now.

No holds barred.

I wanted it dirty and aggressive.

The way we'd just fought was how I wanted us to make love; it wasn't to be anything but a frenzied rush to the finish line. I knew he could take me there, and I intended to seize that chance.

TYEHN

This wasn't how I'd foreseen this going. I'd envisioned her angrily throwing insults at me, and rightly so, for hours to come. In fact, I'd anticipated needing to grovel for days on end, if not weeks.

Yet here we were, rolling around, the two of us tumbling about as we tried to determine who'd be on top. Quite literally.

I was fighting for dominance, my natural personality making me want to take ownership of her; I wanted her to submit to me, just as she'd done when I'd pinned her down.

But Maki was anything but predictable.

Nor did she care for what I wanted. I knew she could take me to the most earth-shattering climax, however she wasn't going to do it by listening to what *my* body wanted. Maki was going to follow her instincts, and in turn, I'd get the fix I also craved.

Her delicate figure was dwarfed against mine, the tight curves of her body contrasting nicely against the rugged muscles of my broad physique.

There were still plenty of garments between the two of us, but as we thrashed about, gyrating against each other in fervent lust. As we went, the items lessened. Soon she'd be naked. Soon she'd be mine, pressed against my bare, green skin.

I longed to melt into her.

As her pelvis rose up to meet me, I landed kisses along her collarbone. Tiny murmurs erupted from her rosy lips, the way they sounded sweeter than the most divine music. People could live a thousand years and they'd never hear delights as intoxicating as her moans. They rose and fell in time to my caress.

Every time my lips brushed her skin, every second of my tongue poking from my mouth to lick her, it all triggered breathy groans.

"You drive me mad." I breathed, desperate for her to know my insatiable appetite. Maki giggled, though her eyes still maintained the hardness of anger.

"If you think that, you should try being around you."

It sounded like a joke, but I knew better. To show that I understood her jibes, I nipped at her sensitive skin, her body trembling at the sharp, sweet impact.

I was tired of this cat and mouse chase now.

I needed more. I *demanded* more.

Lifting my bulky frame onto my hands, I gripped the edges of my top and rolled it away from my body. Her hands instantly suctioned to my bare flesh; the way she stroked gave away her hunger. She was playing coy, pretending to be in control, but I could tell she wanted to fall apart.

Discarding my top, I moved to peel back her clothes to reveal the prize that lay underneath. Maki was a beautiful woman no matter what she wore. However, she looked best when she wore nothing except the skin that the creators had given her.

A soft moan escaped from me now as her nipples hardened, shocked to be exposed to the cool air.

I was glad to see she wasn't wearing another layer below— how ravenous I was right now, I'd have likely ripped her underwear from her.

Given how we were still "working through" our problems, destroying her clothes didn't seem like a smart move.

My eyes stared, unwavering, at her bosom. They were small but pert, the perfect size for my hands to engulf and massage.

Some women had heaving breasts, as large as mountains, but Maki was a svelte framed female.

"You're staring..." She purred, amused by how absorbed by her I was.

"I am," I admitted. "You should expect more of that."

Not wanting to distract us further from our passion, I leaned down to clamp my mouth around one of her nipples.

My tongue swirled around the pink flesh and she crumbled beneath me. I peered up to watch as her head tilted, her eyes rolling to the back of her head a little. Seeing how she savored this as much as I did, led me to move from one breast to the other, her waiting nipple eager to feel the wet warmth of my mouth.

I was devouring her, slowly.

Her fingers stroked up my back, her short nails grazing me, causing me to shake with pleasure. My whole body was rocked by her caress. I growled into a moan, struggling to keep steady.

In that moment, I realized there were still too many clothes between us.

Sitting up, my hands went to her trousers. I fiddled at her zipper just as she instinctively went to mine; we were both growing insane from not having access to every inch of one another.

When the last of her buttons popped, unveiling her panties, I swiftly tugged at her trousers. They came away from her legs easily.

Getting mine off however, wasn't as simple.

Begrudgingly, I stood to remove them. It was hard going, my rushed movements making my body sway dangerously as I attempted to take them off as quickly as my hands would allow. Maki tittered with laughter, clearly amused by my clumsiness.

She wouldn't be laughing soon, though.

Before long she'd be baying my name, begging for me to stop because she couldn't take the energy I was bringing.

Then again, if memory served me correctly, she could bring the fire as much as I could.

More so, even. My Maki was a feisty one.

My Maki.

My mate.

It was the first time I'd thought of her like that, yet it fit well.

Now that I'd said it inside my own head, I couldn't ignore how satisfying it felt.

She really was mine, and now I was going to show her how much.

Standing fully naked, I looked down at her and grinned. Her eyes twinkled back at me. I could see how deeply she was moved by what she saw, my growing length hard to ignore.

I reached my arms out, motioning for her to take my hands with her own. She willingly obliged, her anger finally subsiding.

Once they were clasped in mine, I pulled her up so that she was on her feet.

One of her eyebrows arched at me in a quizzical expression — she wasn't sure where this was going. It made me grin all the more.

I spun her around before she could ask, then bent her over. She folded gracefully, her hands easily able to touch her own toes.

Coming up behind her, my crotch lined up nicely with her behind, my skin against hers an electrifying experience. Especially as I could feel her wetness seeping from between her thighs. She smelled incredible. I licked my lips, savoring the scent.

Placing my hands on her behind, I pulled her towards me. My shaft nestled snugly between her legs, her lips slightly open and waiting for me.

She held her breath in anticipation and, to my surprise, I did the same.

We'd been here before, yet it felt like the first time all over again.

True, I hadn't had her like this, but that didn't make much difference — I could fuck her in the same position for the rest of our lives and it'd never get old. Maki incited too much passion from me for it to ever be dull sex.

Taking my hard cock in hand, I lined it up with her

opening, making sure to teasingly rub up and down before easing myself inside.

As my head felt the ridges of her entrance envelope me, I nearly lost all sense of self. She felt amazing. Unlike any other woman I'd been with.

My exploration of her depths was slow at first, my aim to take my time, make her wait… make her beg. But I found it hard to stick to that plan.

When she wiggled her ass further into me, I decided I didn't care much for soft and slow beginnings. It needed to be as rough as my feelings for her.

If the last few days had taught me much, it was that I was consumed by her in every sense, for good or bad. It was ugly, it was intense, it was a part of me I had no control over anymore.

"Mmmmm, Tyehn… yes…" Maki whispered my name through labored moans, the way she sighed between each word adding to the beauty of her abilities. She was a woman who knew her body.

It allowed her to appreciate what it could do, both to herself and to the people she was with. It was what made being inside of her so euphoric: she knew herself comfortably, thus allowing her to embrace and adapt.

I wanted to spend hours like this. It would be amazing to while away the time deep inside her pussy, either with my tongue or fingers — or both — and then back to using my cock. But time wasn't on our side. It never was.

We knew time was short, but that didn't take away from our moment together. As I strummed my fingers against her clit, my length pounded into her. I was sure to keep a steady, even pace, right up until she started rocking wildly.

She was there, I could feel it. Exerting more pressure, I matched my fingers with my thrusts.

"Ohhhh, oh shit, Tyehn...!" I loved how she cussed as she came. It was so fitting for her, so right for her personality and no nonsense attitude. But I didn't have time to be amused, because I was soon exclaiming my own mix of words as her walls milked me dry.

"Maki, reck... oh, oh, reck..." I couldn't think. Couldn't *speak*. The two of us were foul mouthed, lustful creatures, unable to think of any other words suited to the intensity of our lovemaking.

Once again, the sense of matching one another perfectly came to the fore of my mind.

Emptied of my load, I rolled backward, taking her with me. Although I left the warmth of her between finishing and landing on my back, it was still wonderful to feel her glistening flesh against me.

Panting at one another, Maki turned over so that she was on top facing me. My legs opened so that she could slot in between them.

We stared for a while, though my hands couldn't remain still even though our mouths could. I played with her hair as I gazed into her rich, golden brown eyes.

"I truly am sorry for how I behaved, Maki," I pleaded with her with more than my words. "I was a fool. I shouldn't have ever treated you like there was something wrong with you — there isn't. There never could be. Please, please forgive me." I wasn't above begging, not for a woman like her.

Maki smiled at me, finally. It had taken some time to break through, so much so that I'd started to panic. "You idiot. Of course, I forgive you, just never do that dumb shit again. Deal?"

"Deal."

MAKI

Last night was still playing out inside my head. My own private film. Whenever I wanted to immerse myself in the memories of his touch, of his breath on my neck right before we climaxed.

That should have been enough to keep me sated, but I was never one to settle. Not even when it was good enough for everyone else.

I'd always try for more.

At least, I would have done, if it hadn't been for Teyhn and his team wanting us to head back out to the EcoBright site in the Sika Jungle again.

I appreciated that it made sense to return there, given how much of an epicenter for trouble it had been of late, however I much preferred the idea of spending more time with Tyehn. Preferably with him naked.

On top of me…

"The pair of you need to get a room." Jalok moaned. "Or at least go back and get that bike of Maki's and ride off somewhere private."

"Vhrex is bringing back the bike this evening when he goes with Sylor to retrieve the shuttle," Tyehn said. "And we did get a room."

"I think they did 'get that room' really hard last night, isn't that right you two?" Cazak chuckled at our embarrassed looks, both Tyehn and myself not sure what to do with ourselves.

I wasn't ashamed of our lovemaking, far from it, but I didn't want it to be the only topic of discussion.

"Will you two lay off of it, you've been on all morning with this." Tyehn rolled his eyes, but there was a smugness to his actions — he was enjoying being able to say that I was his.

It made me beam, both inwardly and outwardly, to know he was happy for others to know. Not that it was possible to keep anything from this group.

Nearing Sika, an ungodly racket drew all of our attention, the joy of our jokes soon dispersing like morning mist. The noise invading our ears wasn't normal, it didn't fit with the jungles of this region.

Tyehn nodded to the others, with Sk'lar motioning in agreement. As one, all five of them charged on ahead; Tyehn's hand had been on his sword as he'd moved past me. I prepared myself too, though I didn't have the might of a large sword to go swinging about—

Now isn't the time for jokes, Maki.

I chastised myself while I followed them, my light frame easily able to keep up with them.

When I barged through a dense undergrowth of foliage after them, I came to a halt as suddenly as they had. Initially I couldn't see what they were watching with mixed curiosity and worry. But when I peeked past Tyehn, I soon spotted their cause for concern.

In front of us were a small but able-bodied group of possessed, tirelessly digging over the earth.

Some of them had broken away to destroy large portions of the jungle, though why they were doing this none of us could say.

If they were searching for something in the ground, why did they need to attack anything above ground level?

Before we'd get a chance to ask them — not that I suspected they'd be capable of reasoning — they noticed us. I'd expected them to attack, but instead they fled.

Tyehn went to give chase, but Sk'lar called for him to stop his pursuit.

"They're no threat. If they wanted to fight, they'd have moved on us." I was inclined to agree, though I kept my mouth closed for now.

"But what were they doing?" Tyehn asked tersely. "And what was EcoBright doing out there?"

"That's what I wanna know too!" I exclaimed. "Someone authorized them because I got a job to monitor them. But I have no idea what they were doing."

I pushed past him then, my aim to set as many probes into the earth as I could before whatever they were looking for was lost.

If they were tracking an energy signature, that could rapidly increase and decrease depending on multiple variables. This is what caused me to act with haste, I didn't want to miss any data.

Whatever the EcoBright team was looking for, I wasn't sure it was entirely innocent. Something malevolent was going on and it was aimed against the Puppet Master. I couldn't prove it. But I knew I wasn't wrong.

None of them tried to stop me. They merely watched as I rushed about taking little devices from my pack and then bedding them down into the ground.

Once I had a good number of them scattered across the site, I then took out some specimen vials too. I could collect a few samples while I was here; it paid to be diligent.

Stepping back to observe my handiwork thus far, I

was plagued by all the reasons why they could be digging.

None of them were pleasant.

Going off of what we'd experienced *and* what the Puppet Master had said, there was no way these possessed were doing anything good. Arguably, that's what made this so tense right now: they could be doing anything, all equally sinister as the next.

Seeing as how my mind was eager to torment me with more wild theories, I was happy to see my devices ready with their initial reports. Going back to them one by one, my elation soon turned to annoyance. By the time I took the final reading, I was shaking with barely contained frustration.

"What's wrong?" Sk'lar enquired.

"There's… nothing. There's nothing there at all." I twisted my face in irritation. "It makes no sense, there *has* to be something…"

I was talking to myself now, my speech muffled and low. Tyehn came over and placed a hand on my shoulder, his eyes crinkling as he gave me a smile.

"We've done all we can here, let's move on." As much as it pained me to agree with him, he was right.

LATER THAT NIGHT, I was still troubled by our journey into the Sika Jungle. We hadn't anticipated running into the possessed, but now that we had, all I could think about was their frenzied faces while they'd dug.

It was bugging me not knowing what they were looking for.

And with the scans still coming up empty, I was at a loss at what else to do.

"Still getting to you, huh?" Tyehn asked as he settled down on the couch next to me. I shook my head, exasperated.

"I know it's silly,"

"I didn't say that." He quickly pointed out.

"But it's driving me mad that the scans are all normal — they wouldn't be digging there if it was normal, everyday, run of the mill dirt."

Tyehn shifted so that he was fully turned to look at me now; his face told me he thought I needed to let it go. Even if he tried to deny it, it was etched into his features. I sighed.

"I'm annoying you, aren't I?" I probed, the focus of my ire moving from the possessed to him. Instantly he became more guarded, readying himself for a stinging attack. It made me madder seeing him react to me like that — I didn't like being painted as an unreasonable, hysterical woman!

However, if I was logical about it, I understood why

he expected that of me: I was known for going from hot to cold at lightning speeds.

"You're not, no. But," My eyes narrowed into small slits as he said this. "I think you're overthinking it, Maki."

"How, how can you say that?" I couldn't believe the nerve of him.

"I'm saying it because your scans are normal — if there's nothing showing up, you can't work miracles."

"I know that, Tyehn, but I fail to believe they just decided to get down onto their hands and knees and play in the dirt. Does that sound plausible to you!" My voice was rising to dangerous levels, Tyehn was braced for impact and buckled up ready.

"I mean, you never know, the Ancient Enemies could like sensory play." I gawked at him.

"You did *not* just say that."

"I really did."

He pretended to bow his head in shame and, for the moment, I was free of my worries. They were still there, and they would be for the rest of the night, however I was now able to laugh about it a little.

Not too much, mind, as there was still something unnerving about what we'd witnessed. Nonetheless, for the time being, I had better ways to occupy my mind.

I snuggled into Teyhn and rested my head on his chest. It felt good to be close to him once more. And while the same animalistic thoughts crept in to tempt me, all I wanted to do was be in his arms. There was a simplicity to it that I needed this evening. If I kept that simplicity close, I was able to hold back the niggling fears I had about the Ancient Enemies plans...

They planned something big.

I knew it.

Could feel it.

It made me tense at the idea of it, all of me unable to relax now that they'd gripped my mind once again. I prayed we'd soon be rid of their wickedness, but somehow I felt that was wishful thinking.

"Try to relax, Maki." Tyehn murmured while he played with my hair.

If only he knew how badly I wanted to do just that.

I longed for nothing else.

And he was just the person to help me with that.

I grinned, as I reached for his waistband.

TYEHN

It'd been several days since I apologized to Maki and we sort of made our relationship official.

Several days of reconciling my idiocy and realizing that my mistrust was not with her, but with myself and my fear that I would be unable to handle that part of her past.

I was grateful for Dax's help with what had quickly become labeled 'The Tyehn Excuse.'

I had great friends and teammates.

This morning, we had been called into Rouhr's office for a new assignment. "We have reports of a new compound in the mountains to the west. Some people have reported that it is an anti-alien compound, one of the nasty ones. I want you to investigate and report. Do not engage unless in self-defense, and then only enough for a tactical retreat. We don't want any extra deaths on our hands if possible."

"Sir," Sk'lar spoke up. "Do you really anticipate us being able to act in non-deadly fashion?"

Rouhr looked older than I remembered. He was not dealing with the stress of everything so well, I thought, quietly, to myself. He ran a hand through his hair and leaned back in his desk chair. "I anticipate you following orders, Sk'lar. But, if things get out of control, I want you to do what's necessary to get out of there, but try not to make a mess of things."

"Understood, sir. Is there any more intel about the compound?"

"No. We do have satellite imagery that confirms there are people out there, but our information comes from unsubstantiated reports that they're anti-alien. Since they haven't deigned to check in with anyone or ask for assistance, there is some validity to the reports."

"Okay." With that, we exited the General's office and made our way to the armory where Phin was in charge that day.

"Non-lethal rounds? Are you sure?" he asked when Sk'lar asked for them.

He nodded. "It's required. We're not to kill, just in case."

Phin shook his head in disbelief. "Okay. Non-lethal rounds, coming up. You," he said pointing at me. "Help me load the clips. The rest of you can grab your weapons."

I spent the next ten minutes helping Phin load up the clips with non-lethal rounds while the others retrieved their weapons, checked them, and armored up. Jalok took over for me so I could do the same. He tossed me my bag of clips as I finished strapping on my armor. "Ready?" he asked.

"Let's do it," I answered.

We made our way to the airfield and then to the shuttle where Navat and Cazak got into the cockpit and started the launch procedures.

"So, how are you and Maki holding up?" Sk'lar asked.

I shot my head up to look at him.

He had never asked me anything personal before. While the five of us were a team, Sk'lar wasn't the type to fraternize with us.

He had gotten a little better since his relationship with Phryne, but in general he was still aloof and separated.

"Uh, we're, uh, we're doing good, I think," I answered.

Jalok snorted. "That means he doesn't have a recking clue. It's too new for him to know anything."

He wasn't wrong. We had only been officially together for a few days, and I wasn't certain that we were anything more than just two people that had slept together and shared a few laughs.

"He'll get there. Remember how our relationships started? We weren't terribly sure at the beginning either," Sk'lar commented. "Now, at least for me, I'm pretty sure that Phryne and I are doing well. What about you and Dottie?"

"We're still good, but she's dealing with some people still looking at her as if she's violating some sort of code or something."

"How is she dealing with that?" I asked.

"She's essentially telling them all to go reck themselves. She's enjoying her time with me, at least that's what she tells me all the time," Jalok said with a devilish grin.

He didn't know how to keep his private life private sometimes.

We all cracked jokes and told stories as we flew, enjoying one another's company for the three hour flight far out into the mountains. "Three minutes," Navat called from the front.

We were instantly serious, ready for anything that could come our way.

Except, we weren't.

The shuttle landed and we came out, weapons ready, but pointed down to avoid any confusion.

Coming towards us were ten people, five men and five women. One man in particular stepped forward.

"Hello. My name is Logan. Might I ask who you are?" He was a middle aged man with a balding head, light gray hair on the sides, but still physically imposing.

His short sleeve shirt revealed muscles that were not for show, as well as a deep tan that showed he worked a lot outside.

His clean cut face held a smile that seemed genuine while his voice carried a deep bass that seemed as if it would shake the bones if he ever got loud.

Sk'lar stepped forward, his weapon dangling from his shoulder. "My name is Sk'lar. I am commander of this strike team. My men are Jalok, Cazak, Navat, and Tyehn," he introduced each of us and pointed us out. We all stepped forward at the mention of our names, putting us a step closer to Sk'lar in case anything happened.

"Pleasure meeting you," Logan said with a friendly nod and wave. "Now, if you would be so kind as to explain why you are here."

"Well, we've received reports of a settlement being made out here and we were curious as to whether or not you needed any assistance, supplies, or anything else to help you in the establishment of your home."

"Ah. Well, thank you for your offers. However, we are not inclined to accept help from you."

"And why is that, Logan?" Sk'lar asked.

Logan looked around and so did I. We weren't alone.

We were surrounded by several dozen men and women, each one looking like they were armed. I coughed quietly and motioned around. While we didn't reach for our weapons, we did move our hands closer to them.

"I see," Sk'lar said in resignation. "So, this is an anti-alien establishment."

"In a sense," said Logan. "But not in the way that you think. We're not hostile, simply wish to be left alone is all. You see, Mr. Sk'lar, we're not particularly comfortable around your kind. Not that we wish you harm or anything like that. We just want to be on our own, is all."

"So, you're not out here plotting our deaths or coming up with ways to drive us off the planet?" Navat asked.

Logan looked past Sk'lar at Navat, who was standing right next to me. "Navat, correct?"

He nodded.

"No, friend Navat. While I'm sure some of us might be, because I can't read everyone's minds, but no, we're not here trying to build an army to drive you away," he answered. "I can promise you that. We are here simply to be on our own, to raise our families and to live in peace. Maybe someday we can come back down and learn to live in tandem with you, or at least as friendly neighbors, but today is not that day."

Sk'lar stepped forward, his hands far away from his weapon. "Then, may I extend an official offer of assistance, if you were to ever need it, and a sincere hope that one day we will be able to speak again, as friends." He extended his hand out.

Logan stepped forward, a smile on his face and accepted Sk'lar's handshake. "Perhaps one day, we can do this in friendly greeting." They shook hands and parted, both turning around at the same time. Logan raised a hand and I watched as the people around us seemingly vanished, several of them coming out from behind rock outcroppings and bushes a minute later.

Sk'lar walked up to us. "Let's go. They're not bad people, and they were simply prepared to defend themselves is all. Move."

We turned around and made our way back to the shuttle, Navat and Cazak jogging ahead to prep the shuttle. "Tyehn, bring up the rear, just in case."

"Aye," I said. I turned around and backed my way towards the shuttle, making sure that no one was going to try anything. I spotted a few people watching us, but they all waved as I began to board. I gave a slight wave in return and kept an eye on things as the shuttle door closed.

"That was interesting," Cazak called back from the cockpit.

"A little more than interesting," Jalok said. "Want to lay down odds that they were lying?"

"Stop it," Sk'lar ordered. "We have to at least attempt to trust them. Not everyone is automatically evil."

"Really?"

"Come on, Jalok," I stepped in. "You really think that they're bad people? Our respective species hated one another before the Xathi. We learned to trust one another to the point that we've become friends. Why not them?"

Jalok opened his mouth to respond, then stopped. "Okay. You're right. Maybe they are just wanting to be on their own. We should try to respect that, I guess." He sat down. "I just don't think we should blindly believe in their words, though."

"And we won't," I said. "We'll be careful. But, we can't just automatically think that everyone is immediately an enemy just because they say they don't like us. I still don't like our command structure back home, but I trust in them to fight the Xathi."

"Good words, Tyehn," Sk'lar said.

It was a bit disheartening to know that these people didn't like us, but it was encouraging that they were willing to accept us as a part of life, and instead of fighting us, they simply moved away so they could come to grips with us as part of their reality.

Maybe things weren't going to be as bad as we had once thought.

But I wouldn't bet on it.

MAKI

I can't see with my own eyes. *I know that they're mine, attached to me, yet what I'm seeing isn't through my pupils but ones governed by someone else.*

All that's before me is familiar, yet I'm unable to break through the barriers inside my own mind. I see faces staring, they seem to know me, but I'm acting against my will.

I'm not in control anymore. My hands flex to the command of someone else, my body starting to transition... Somewhere inside of me demands that I fight, fight until I can't stand it any longer.

"Oh my god," I breathed, my eyes snapping open.

I was back with the Puppet Master, its tendrils curling around me, tentatively trying to soothe me as I became aware of my surroundings.

It had been a dream. No, a memory. Even though I'd

lived it, and had just seen it for myself, it still didn't seem real.

"Memory retrieval can be difficult, the transition into one's deepest thoughts often causes discomfort. I'm sorry." The sincerity I felt from such a brief and simple sentence was incredibly overwhelming; I'd conversed with people for much of my life and never felt genuine empathy from them.

Yet this gigantic plant oozed understanding from every vine that grew and stretched away from its body.

A lot of the human population could stand to gain a great deal from listening to the teachings of this wise creature.

And yet few of them would ever come to bask in the formidable serenity of his presence.

I absentmindedly brushed my hand along one of its vines, the need to be physically connected to one another difficult to ignore.

I knew Tyehn would still prefer caution from me, but considering all that the Puppet Master was helping me accomplish, I lacked the reservations he still held.

"There's no need to apologize, I knew it would be an experience, I just appreciate your help." It was my turn for sincerity now.

"Helping you realize your past helps me as much as it does you, it's a mutual partnership."

I gave an empty laugh, though I didn't mean it

sound as careless as it did. It wasn't that I didn't appreciate the Puppet Master's honesty, just that it would have been nicer if he'd been more pragmatic with it.

Sometimes he oozed it, others he was nothing save a logical, all knowing entity. The two were interchangeable and deeply connected, but that didn't mean he couldn't switch from one to the other.

Much like many other living creatures, the Puppet Master had multiple facets to his personality.

"I promised myself I wouldn't do this," I began to explain, rather unnecessarily, seeing as how nobody was there to scold me. "but I have questions about your past... and about *who* you are."

"You who know I am."

"Okay, poor wording on my part — I mean, is it weird to think of you as a 'he' or are you more an 'it'? Just the latter sounds really mean, as if I don't see you as a living creature, which you most definitely are." My shoulders shrugged as I spoke, my body trying to pass off my inquisitiveness as unimportant; it could be answered or ignored, I was cool with it either way. Except I wasn't because I *needed* to know more.

"You can refer to me however you wish, whatever helps make our time together easier for you to understand."

It wasn't what I was looking for, but I already felt my mind leaning toward addressing him as a person.

As a *male*. I didn't know why I felt the need to gender a plant, however I was doing it whether I liked it or not. It was almost as if my mind couldn't comprehend a sentient being of this magnitude without assigning it a gender—

And you just had to make it male. Nice one, Maki! I was full of sass today, and all of it was aimed at myself.

"So, my next question, what about your past — do you remember much of it, what was it like, has the world changed a lot since then?" I was speeding on ahead, as always.

However, I sensed that the Puppet Master was becoming used to my chaotic thought processes, much like a mentor does with their student. A steady rhythm is formed, one that both parties are able to follow.

"My past is almost forgotten to me now, much like yours was to you," Began his explanation, the way he filled my head still a sensation I had yet to get used to. It wasn't as shocking anymore, but I still found myself in awe of being able to hear him. *"The centuries I've been alive, I slept through a lot of the civilizations that have lived here, using my subconscious to tend to the creation and sustainability of the world they inhabited."*

"That's, well, that's remarkable — you know that, right? I mean, you must do. To be able to do all of that and not even be awake. Wow, I'd get so much shit done if I could live like that."

I was smiling at the Puppet Master then, amused by my own jokes, but I was also appreciative that he didn't think me foolish for sharing them. His features formed a gentle, transcendent smile as he observed me.

"I suppose it is remarkable, though for me, it's as natural as the air around us. I can't do anything other than what I've been designed to do."

"But how did you manage to keep track of everything? That's a lot of balls to be juggling."

"I can concentrate on several tasks at any one time, just as I'm doing right now. Even though I'm talking with you, I'm also holding a conversation with six other people."

"Six? Seriously? Whoa." I didn't know any other phrase that could illustrate how amazed I was at the scope of his reach.

It seemed silly to be so surprised by the awesomeness of a creature as fantastical as this. Yet on the other hand, it was also easy to appreciate why most of us naturally reacted this was: it was abnormal to us.

An unknown.

Out of our predictable bubble of reality. Space travel, aliens, other worlds — they'd all seemed abnormal and otherworldly in the past, yet here we were, on a planet filled with humans and aliens, side by side. I mused whether one day people would think of the Puppet Master as normal, a part of the planet's furnishings.

"Would you like to know a secret, Maki?"

I arched my brows, unsure of what he could possibly share with me that he felt it important to disclose now. Would it be a secret about his past, about the possessions and the Ancient Enemies?

The list was quite endless, my mind allowing the theories to snowball while I waited. I nodded my head, my breath catching in my throat as I froze on the spot. It was similar to readying yourself for an ascension, or so I imagined.

"Your relationship with Tyehn, it's unique. Even in spite of the differences you two have, which at times can prove challenging to overcome, you're now bonded together in a way you could never have imagined. And part of that is because of our interactions." Something like a ripple of laughter flowed through me. *"I rather like being a part of that."*

I became lost for words.

Not because I feared that I cared for Tyehn due to having met a plant, but because it made sense to me that it had changed our dynamic.

It wasn't possible to stand in the presence of such a being and come out unchanged; if anyone was capable of doing that, I doubted they were of this world.

Tyehn and I would have become close regardless of our coming here, of that I felt certain.

Nevertheless, we wouldn't have been able to grow

together, to be nurtured as a couple, without the connection of the Puppet Master. By bringing the two of us here, by needing to speak with us, he'd orchestrated a chain of events that couldn't be undone.

He'd exposed my darkest secret, and Tyehn's lingering fears about the hybrids, and made us lance the wound before it festered.

We were stronger because of it.

Turning my eyes down to the earthy, moss-covered ground, I was nervous to share my feelings. And yet, I needed to voice them. I wanted someone to know how I was feeling, how deeply my emotions had taken hold of me.

"I care for Tyehn so much, more than I thought I ever would. When I first met him, I'd expected us to get along, eventually, but never like this. Not to the point where I prefer my days and nights to be spent with him." As I came to the end of my admission, it felt good to have it off of my chest. I felt unburdened.

"Your bond with him is permanent. Even if the hands of time change it, you'll always be drawn to him the same way he is to you, your fates forever locked together. It's woven into the fabric of the world."

I shook my head, dismayed but entertained at the same time. "Tyehn will love hearing this if he ever finds out."

My humor was a means for me to deflect, and it worked.

Kind of. Although I could pass my feelings off as casual to myself, doing so to the Puppet Master wasn't so easy. I didn't like the idea of lying to him, not when we'd started to form a bond of our own.

"I truly care for him," I whispered, my eyes peering into the Puppet Master's own reflective irises. "I care for him, and it scares me half to death."

EPILOGUE : TYEHN

This truly was a beautiful city. Walking down the streets in the evening light, I enjoyed the natural feel of the city and how, even covered in snow, you could see where the people of the city tried to keep things as close to nature as they could.

I could see where there were smaller plants covered to protect from the cold. I could feel the grass under my feet where the people tried to keep the sidewalks as natural as possible.

The more time I spent here, the more I liked it here.

The people were fairly nice, as well. Many of them nodded or waved at me as I walked down the streets.

There were still some that crossed the street to get away from me, or scowled at me when I passed them and attempted to greet them, but they weren't as numerous as in some other places I had travelled to.

The bag of groceries I carried in my arm was an odd accessory to go along with my armor, my three handguns, my sword, two knives, and my rifle slung over my shoulder.

To be honest, I was surprised as many people smiled and greeted me as they did. I didn't discount that I had been here often and the people had started to get to know me, but it still surprised me that while I was decked out in full battle gear, they were still cordial and polite.

Maybe it was *because* I was in full gear they were polite, but their smiles looked genuine enough.

"Ho, Tyehn," someone called out to me. I looked over to see an older gentleman that I knew who worked at the Command Center in Nyheim.

"Thomas," I called back. I double checked the traffic, then crossed the street to greet my friend. "My friend. How are you?"

He extended his hand out to me and we shook hands as he answered. "I'm doing well, for the most part. My knee is acting up a little, but the medicine helps."

"I'm both glad and sorry to hear that. Glad that the medicine is helping, but sad that your knee is in a state that you need it."

"Thank you, Tyehn. What are you up to?"

"Nothing much," I answer with a slight shrug. "About to go make dinner for a friend."

He arched an eyebrow at me and fit me with a smile. "Really? And, is this friend of yours someone special?"

I nodded. "She is."

"Good. We should all have that special friend that we want to make dinner for. I'm actually on my way over for a special dinner of my own."

"Oh?"

"Yes. Sasha invited me over for a dinner. I mean, Sasha's a fantastic cook, so how could I pass up an amazing meal?"

"And the fact that you and Sasha are highly compatible, to use your word, helps, doesn't it?" I smirked.

He smiled and looked away for a moment, looking out towards the soon to be setting sun. "True. I haven't felt this way about anyone since Tracy passed away a decade ago, so it feels good. Don't let this one slide through your fingers. Life is far too short and unpredictable to take for granted my friend."

There was a tinge of unhappiness in his voice, one that I recognized from our conversations about his past as we got to know one another. "No worries, Thomas. I'll do my best to hold on to her."

"Good. Now, what were you planning on making this amazing woman that's captured your attention?"

I looked down in the bag and suddenly felt a little self-conscious about my choices. "Well, it's a meal that my mother used to make for me as a child. I believe that the human word for it is 'stew.' I figured, maybe if I share something from my past that always made me feel good, it would be a good start."

"Smart move," he said, then checked his watch. "Oh, I better go or I'll be late. And, if you're making a stew, you're going to need time to get it to cook properly."

"Very true. Good seeing you, my friend."

"You as well. Enjoy." He shook my hand and restarted his travels down the street as I restarted my own. It didn't take long before I was at Maki's door, my hand hovering in front of her door as I hesitated.

Finally, I knocked. It took a few moments, but Maki finally opened the door. "Tyehn. Hey, come in, come in." She let me into her apartment, papers strewn all over her couch, her living room table, and the dining room table as well.

"Everything okay?" I asked.

"Huh?" she looked at me, then looked at all the papers. "Oh, yeah. Yeah, just going over the soil sample results I got. There's a lot of stuff here that isn't normal when compared to other samples and I'm just trying to see what the differences are. So far, the stuff on the dining room table are the comparisons, the ones on the couch are the control samples, and the ones on the living room table are the abnormalities."

"Anything to worry about?" I asked as I set the bag of groceries in the kitchen, then turned back to look at Maki and her work.

"I don't think so," she said. "I think it's more just information that I'm not used to seeing. That part of the jungle had recently gone through some regrowth, so maybe it's just particulates that show that regrowth. Then again, maybe it had something to do with that crazy place we were in. I'll figure it out."

Then she looked past me to the bag. "What's that?"

I blushed a bit. "I thought that maybe I could make you dinner."

"What? Really?" She looked to be in shock. "You want to make *me* dinner?"

"Why not?"

"I-I, I don't know. Guess I'm not used to people wanting to do something nice for me."

I fit her with a look of disbelief as I removed my gear and placed it off to the side. "Really? Why do I find that so hard to believe? You're beautiful, funny, adventurous, intelligent, and whatever adjective that I don't have the knowledge of that compliments you."

She shrugged to try to hide her own blushing cheeks. "Yeah, well, when you're constantly busy with work and a non-stop adrenaline junkie, it's hard to have people around you that are willing to do nice things."

"And I call, what's the word you humans like to use so much? Oh, 'bullshit.' You have friends." I started taking the food out of the bag and began prepping the food. "Do you have a large pot?"

"Cabinet at your left knee. And, yes, I do have friends. I'm not denying that, and we do things together and stuff. Just, I guess I haven't had someone that was willing to do things for me just for the sake of doing things, you know?"

I stood up after getting the pot out. "No, not really. Then again, I'm part of a military strike team and if we don't have complete trust and faith in one another, then we struggle to work well in the field. So, we've always made a point to try to be brothers and do things for one another in order to maintain the camaraderie and trust."

I opened a drawer looking for a kitchen knife. "Two drawers over," Maki said. "What are you making me?"

"Well, it's a meal that my mother used to make me when I was a child. I'm hoping I cook it the same, since you don't offer me the exact same ingredients that I get from home."

"You're really making me something your mom made you?"

I nodded.

"Thank you. Did you need some help?"

"Sure," I said. "If you want to cut up these round things here, um…"

"Onions?"

"Yes."

We spent the next few minutes cutting up the vegetables and then we started searing the meat. "Smells good," she said. "What kind of spices did you put on it?"

"Uh, the lady at the shop called it lemon togarashi."

"Smells good."

"You said that already," I teased.

"Yeah, yeah. Shut up," she said as she stuck her tongue out at me. I stuck my tongue out at her in return.

"How long will this take?"

"Hmm, maybe an hour," I answered. "Why?"

She shrugged. "Just curious how long I have to wait for dinner, that's all. I mean, you want to feed me food and you're gonna make me wait, you know. I'm just saying, seems a little unfair to make me wait for dinner."

"Oh, really? And when were you planning on eating if I hadn't come over?"

"Um, well, you see—"

"Yep. Now, shut up and let me cook. Or, let me put

everything in the pot and let it cook itself for an hour. What I love about this dish, is you can't srell it up."

"Wow, you're a real connoisseur of food and language, aren't you?"

"Ha. Ha."

She smiled at me as I finished putting everything in the pot and turned on the stove. I made my way out of the kitchen and into the living room where she was cleaning up her papers. "Alright, where do we put these," I asked.

"Just on the table," she answered. "So, what now?" She sat on the couch and patted the seat next to her.

"We have an hour," I purred, pulling her onto my lap.

She laughed, and the bond between us tightened, a near physical tug in my chest.

My Maki.

My mate.

"You have a plan for that time?" she teased, plump lips a hair's breath away from my own.

"That time, and forever," I answered, and then my lips did the rest of the talking.

Turns out you can srell up stew if you ignore it for four hours.

But it was worth it.

Entirely.

LETTER FROM ELIN

I have the feeling Maki is going to keep Tyehn on his toes… and he's going to love every minute of it!

Next up, it's the start of a new year on the Conquered World, and party girl Sibyl is about to get a rude awaking.

Luckily for her, Cazak will be there.

Together the two of them will have to face the growing threat - even when it's at the heart of her family…

Keep reading for a sneak peak!

XOXO,

Elin

PLEASE DON'T FORGET TO LEAVE A REVIEW!

Readers rely on your opinions, and your review can help others decide on what books they read. Make sure your opinion is heard and leave a review where you purchased this book!

Don't miss a new release! You can sign up for release alerts at both Amazon and Bookbub:

bookbub.com/authors/elin-wyn

amazon.com/author/elinwyn

For a free short story, opportunities for advance review copies, release news and the occasional cat picture, please join the newsletter!

https://elinwynbooks.com/newsletter-signup/

And don't forget the Facebook group, where I post sneak peeks of chapters and covers!

https://www.facebook.com/groups/ElinWyn/

CAZAK: SNEAK PEEK

SIBYL

"Three!" The entire crowd shouted in one voice.

"Two!" The energy in the room was electric, a thousand voices oiled by alcohol turning into a chorus. I let a smile spread across my lips as I focused on the holographic screen behind the DJ, and held my flute of champagne up in the air.

"One!"

The whole crowd went nuts.

The retractable ceiling started sliding back to reveal a starry sky, and the whistle of a hundred fireworks climbing up into the night blended with the chorus. When the first fireworks went off, an explosion of light pushing away the darkness in the sky, I joined the others and cried out at the top of my lungs.

"Happy New Year!"

The room, which had its lights dimmed for the countdown, was now filled with the bright colors of the fireworks. They went off for almost ten minutes, covering the sky in colorful teardrops, and every single person in the club watched the show with a kind of wide-eyed amazement. It had been a while since Kaster had seen such a celebration and, after a couple of rough years, I figured the entire city needed something like this.

I knew I did.

"Let's get this party started," the DJ screamed into his hovering microphone. He pushed a few buttons on his control panel, and the holographic screen behind him lit up once more. The neon colors there ebbed and flowed with a rhythm that matched the music, the pounding bass making my chest vibrate. Placing my empty champagne flute on the counter, I headed into the dance floor and brought both my hands up. Running my fingers through my hair, I swayed my hips to the rhythm. I whipped my hair back and forth, enjoying the vibrancy of the night, and let a wide smile take over my lips.

There was nothing better than a good party.

"Enjoying yourself, aren't you?" Someone screamed

into my ears, but I still had a hard time making out the words. I turned to see a handsome young man stand beside me, the sleeves of his white button up shirt rolled up his sleeves. He had the kind of grin on his lips that meant trouble, and there was a glint in his eyes that told me I had snagged all of his attention.

"What?"

"Enjoying yourself, aren't you?" He repeated, and this time I replied with a wink. Facing him, I ran my hands down the side of my body and dragged my teeth over my bottom lip. I kept my eyes on his as I danced, and it didn't take long before he closed the distance between us. My father would've hated to see me dancing with a stranger, but what the hell. Some dancing and innocent flirting never really killed anyone, right? No harm in living life and having some fun.

"What do you say we grab some shots?" The guy screamed again, doing his best to talk over the loud music. He pointed toward the corner, where a group of five or six guys was busy downing shot after shot, and I gave him a quick nod.

Grabbing my hand, he led me through the packed dance floor and, somehow, we managed to make our way to the place where his friends were. He motioned at the bartender for two shots and, just a couple of seconds later, I had a small glass pushed into my hands.

"Bottoms up!" I laughed and, without waiting for him, threw my head back and drank it all up. I grimaced as the alcohol made its way down my throat, but I didn't let that stop me. Once another shot somehow appeared in front of me, I reached for it and drank it up.

"Slow down," the man laughed. "You keep that up and you won't last the night."

"I can handle my liquor."

"I can see that."

"Are these your friends?" I asked him, pointing to the group of twenty-somethings surround him. He replied with a nod, and then started naming his friends. They all winked and nodded at me as my new friend introduced them all, but I wasn't really paying attention to any of it. I couldn't hear what their names were and, truth be told, I didn't really care. All I wanted was to dance.

"Sure feels good, huh?"

"What does?" I asked him.

"Look around you," he smiled, waving at the crowd. "Notice anything?"

"Not really," I admitted.

"Not a single alien in here," he laughed. "I can't remember the last place I walked into a party without having to see one of them. Feels great, doesn't it?"

"I don't get it," I frowned. "Are you one of those anti-alien guys?"

"Well, wouldn't you say that it's high time we—"

"I'm gonna dance," I cut him short and, without waiting for his reply, I turned my back to him and slipped back into the crowd. It seemed all everyone wanted to do nowadays was dabble on politics and talk smack about the aliens. Why ruin a good party with such boring conversation?

"Who's your friend?" I heard someone laugh right behind me, and I spun on my heels to see Aman, one of the girls that had come with me. She was rocking back and forth on her heels, her eyes already turning glassy. Still, that didn't seem to stop her from sipping on whatever cocktail she had on her hands. "His friends are cute. Care to introduce me?"

"Nah," I laughed back at her. "They're boring as hell."

"Really?"

"They just wanna talk about aliens and whatever."

"Ugh." Rolling her eyes, she then shook her head. "Let's get out of here then, before this entire party turns into a snooze fest. I know of a club just around the block, and a friend of mine told me they're partying hard in there."

"What are you waiting for?" I grinned. "Lead the way."

We stumbled onto the streets a few minutes later,

the chaos of a New Year's celebration punctuated by loud chants and the laughter of people drinking outside the bars. I followed after Aman as best as I could, but it didn't take a genius to see that I would have to put an end to my night. I was already swaying like a boat during a storm, and the world around me seemed to be spinning too fast for my eyes to keep up.

"You go ahead," I finally said, hands on my knees as I tried to catch my breath. "I think I'm gonna call it a night."

"It's not even two," Aman protested, but I just gave her a sheepish smile. "C'mon, you're not gonna leave me alone, are you? I can't handle all the cute boys by myself, can I?"

"I'm sure you'll manage." Standing straight—at least as much as I could—I ran one hand through my hair and scanned my surroundings, trying to remember where I had left the car. "I think I've just drank too much."

"You're a disappointment, Sibyl," Aman laughed. "C'mon, I'll walk you to your car."

The two of us went through a side avenue, and it didn't take long before I spotted the turquoise sports aircar parked in front of a club. I unlocked the door with my fingerprint, and then climbed inside awkwardly. Sprawled on the back seat, I waved Aman goodbye and told the computer to close the door.

"Take me home," I said, doing my best not to spill dinner all over the leather upholstery. My dad would kill me if that happened.

"*Destination set as: home,*" the car's AI droned in its monotone voice, and the engine came alive with a growl. "*Estimated arrival time: 25 minutes.*" I bounced in my seat as the car pushed its weight off the pavement, and I quickly buckled myself up.

I spent the entire journey with my eyes closed, and I only dared to open them when I became certain dinner would remain in my stomach. I looked out the window to see the quiet suburbs underneath me, the brightly lit centre of Kaster just a flash in the distance, and I rested my forehead against the glass.

A few minutes later and the car started its descent into the gated courtyard of a stately manor. It stopped right in front of the imperial staircase that led the way to the front entrance, and jumped out of the car as silent as cat. A very drunk cat. Even though I was pretty sure someone must've heard the car, I still hoped I'd manage to get inside my bedroom without anyone noticing me.

I held my breath as I opened the front door, and my father's voice immediately boomed from the entrance hall. "Do you have any idea what time it is?" He stood just a few steps away from the door, both hands on his hips as he stared me down. He was wearing a tailored suit that somehow managed to hide the weight he had put on these last few years, an attire he must've chosen for whatever boring party he had to attend. You'd think that the Mayor of Kaster would be livin' it up, but that wasn't the case. More often than not, all my father had to do was take infinite administrative meetings and attend functions so boring I could fall asleep just thinking of them.

"It's...huh...two in the morning," I mumbled, trying to pretend I was sober. It didn't work. Every word I tried to push out of my mouth was as mellow as a caramel that had been left under a summer's sun.

"Are you drunk?"

"It's New Year's," I said. "I've had a few drinks. So what?"

He didn't say anything. He just stared at me, eyes narrowed, and he clenched his fists. He started to shout at me, but I was so damn drunk I couldn't understand a word of what he was saying.

"I'm going to bed," I merely said, and turned my back on him. He kept on shouting as I stumbled up the stairs that led into my bedroom, but I just ignored him. There was something odd about him. Even though he didn't really like my partying habits, my father wasn't really the kind of man to act as angrily as he was right now.

Whatever.

Stepping into my bedroom, I made a beeline straight toward my bed and collapsed on top of the mattress.

I was so drunk I didn't even fall asleep.

I straight up passed out.

CAZAK

I enjoyed working the night shift. It was quiet, simple, peaceful, and the best time for me to sit back and think. The night shift was a great chance for me to get away from the insanity and the stress of the day-to-day comings and goings of our jobs.

Of course, ever since the Xathi were defeated, our jobs had changed. We were no longer strike teams being sent out to conduct covert acts against our enemies. We were now being used for supply runs, security work, and the occasional protection details for whoever might need it.

Like tonight. Tonight, Jalok, Navat, and I were on security detail, helping out the local police force maintain sanity during their New Year's celebrations. I liked New Years celebrations. They were always a time to throw worries and concerns to the side, at least for an evening and celebrate the end of an old year and the beginning on a new one that would hopefully be an improvement over the previous. Then again, it was also a time to throw inhibitions and will power on the back burner in order to enjoy one evening of fun, debauchery, and insanity.

As long as you maintained a semblance of control during your actions. I used to be one of those people that would lose control and just focus strictly on the fun and debauchery. It had cost me as well.

However, after a life-changing moment, followed immediately by a universe-changing moment, I was no longer that person and I was now the one that tried to help control and save people that lost control. That's what we were working on tonight, trying to control insanity.

"Cazak, we got a call," Jalok, my cousin, said as he clicked off his communicator with the police. "They want us at a party near some place called Leverage Tower. While it's not out of hand yet, they are worried that it will be soon, so they want us there to help keep an eye on things."

"Okay, let's go watch people dance in the snow," Navat said with a smile. I turned my head up for a moment and watched as the snow fell through the lights. Dancing in this would have been fun in my younger days. Of course, humans were the only ones that held their New Years celebrations in the middle of winter, the rest of the sane universe held theirs either during spring or just before the summer equinox.

"Drive or jog?" I asked as I turned my head back to the others.

"Jog, it's not far from here," Jalok smiled. He started jogging, Navat and I only a few paces behind. The city was unnaturally beautiful with the holiday decorations, the snow, and the lights. The revelers that were walking and dancing in the streets stayed away from us.

As we jogged, Jalok put his hand up to his ear and spoke to someone. I couldn't hear his words, but when he started jerking his head around in anger, I got the gist of the conversation. "Move it, people are starting to argue and there's some minor physical activity. They're worried it's gonna turn into a fight and we need to get there, now."

We picked up our pace, turning our jog into a run, but not quite a sprint. We were at Leverage Tower within six minutes. As we were arriving, there was a small scuffle happening between two groups of party goers, and I could hear their argument from where we were.

"You fucking alien lover! You're probably pregnant with one of their babies, aren't you?" The current speaker was a large man, not muscular, and he was picking on a young lady, yelling at her. When her date, or just someone trying to help her, stepped forward, the large man pushed him.

I stepped forward and he turned to me.

"Yeah, you, you alien dumb fuck," he growled as he pointed at me. "I asked, what the hell are you looking at? You staring at one of *our* women? You thinking of taking one of *our* women? What, you think we're here to serve you, to get down on our knees and bow down to you?"

"Don't respond," Jalok said quietly. "Let's not provoke them." Then he turned to the crowd. "We're not here for any trouble. We're simply here to ensure that everyone has a good time without anything untoward happening."

"Go fuck yourself," the loud man yelled. He was a young one, possibly mid-twenties, if that. He was dressed very well, with a bright green shirt, dark gray vest, gray tie, and gray slacks. It was an impressive ensemble. Too bad the clothes were filled with an idiot with a big mouth.

"I'm going to apologize for my friend here," I said as I took a step forward. "He forgot to mention that we're working with the local police force and that we have jurisdictional rights to arrest anyone causing trouble. Now, we're simply here to ensure that everyone has a good time and that no one does anything to mess up said good time. Let's simply leave it at that, shall we?"

The human rolled his eyes and stumbled a bit to the side. His friends laughed, but one of them leaned into his ear and started talking, pointing at us. "I know, shut up," Green Shirt snarled. He turned his attention back to us. "It's simple, alien bitch, get the hell off our planet."

"Come on, man. Leave him alone," another one of the men said.

"Shut the fuck up, Eric, or I'll stick your head up his alien ass. You know what? Screw this." Then Green Shirt started walking towards us, almost stomping.

"Don't do this," I said. "It's not going to end well for you."

He was only a few paces away and snarling. His eyes flashed and I knew right there that he was being taken over.

"He's possessed," I warned the others as they raised their weapons. I, instead, let go of mine and let it swing on the strap behind me. "Don't do this," I repeated. "I really don't want to hurt you. Just go back to the party and celebrate."

I stepped a few steps forward, my hands held out to my side, palms out.

This didn't calm him down as I wanted. Instead, it seemed to infuriate him instead. He got within swinging distance and threw a left hook. It was an easy blow to block as he was off-balance, and in his slightly inebriated nature, he didn't have the power that he would have if it was simply anger driving him.

So, I blocked it and pushed him away. His eyes went

wide and he charged me. He tried to tackle me, but I grabbed out, caught his shoulders, spun him around, and pushed him away again. "Please, stop. I warned you that this was not going to go well." I turned back to Jalok and Navat. "When are the police getting here?"

Jalok shrugged.

"Great." I turned back to Green Shirt. He rushed me again. This time, instead of trying to tackle me, he jumped into the air, his knee aimed at my face. I caught him, but his knee connected with my shoulder, driving me off balance as I held him and tried to throw him off me. Instead of merely throwing him off to the side, he was thrown into the side of a trash can. When he shouted out in pain, his friends shouted out in anger and rushed us.

"Koso, Cazak. What did you do?" Navat cursed as he slung his weapon behind him and caught his attacker. Jalok side-stepped his and threw a quick punch to the back of the head.

I shook my own head and turned back towards Green Shirt. He charged, again, but this time he actually caught me off guard. He feinted to my left, then went to my right, except he went low instead of high like I had been expecting. He caught me in the knee, dragging me down to the ground. He climbed on top of me and started throwing punches. I managed to cover up and block most of them, then reached out, caught a punch, and put him into an arm-bar. I pulled and snapped my head up, headbutting him. I rolled him over, pulling his arm behind him and there was a sickening pop from his shoulder.

At his scream, I let go and reached behind me for the handcuffs the police had given us. I snapped them onto one wrist, then onto the other and looked up to see Jalok and Navat standing, their weapons pointed at the rabble rousers and the police finally arriving.

Statements were taken, the three men were taken away, and I was double checked to make sure my knee was fine.

"That was fun," Navat said with a smile.

I let out a bark of laughter, making the others look at me with arched eyebrows. "What?"

"You thought that was fun? I was making a sarcastic comment," Navat said.

I shrugged. "Eh. The night has only just begun. Maybe we'll get to see some more nice cars, or another idiot in nice clothes being possessed."

I knew I wasn't acting like myself, but that's why I loved the night shift. Nothing was normal.

SIBYL

I woke up feeling like a vampire.

The sunlight streaming through the large windows

of my bedroom made my head throb violently, and a wave of nausea took over me as I sat up on the bed. Pinching the bridge of my nose, I sucked in a deep breath and forced my eyelids open.

God, what a hangover.

Groaning, I swung my legs off the bed and walked toward the windows. The sky was of a deep grey, and the courtyard was covered in at least two feet of snow. It was a lovely sight, except the brightness of it all didn't help the throbbing pain in my head. I drew the curtains, momentarily relishing the shadows that embraced me, and ambled toward my ensuite bathroom.

Slowly, I pushed the straps of my dress down my shoulders—I hadn't even bothered to undress last night—and turned the shower on. Two minutes later and a fine mist started taking over the bathroom, and only then did I push my dress down my body and onto the floor. Naked, I stepped inside the shower and threw my head back as the warm water fell against my skin.

There was nothing better than a hot shower after a late night of partying. Now I just needed to munch on some toast, drink a couple or two of coffee, and I'd be good to go. With some luck, I wouldn't even have to take an aspirin.

"Computer, what's the time?" I asked, and the AI system that was part of the manor immediately spoke up in a warm feminine voice.

"*It's half past seven in the morning.*"

It was early then. I tended to get up after lunch whenever I spent the whole night drinking, but it seemed like my body was ready to tackle the first day of the year on a high note. Not that I had much to do. My father was always needling me to find something productive to do, but I felt like I was already productive enough. At least when it came to partying.

Feeling better now, I toweled myself off and put on a pair of ripped jeans and a trendy sweater. I applied some light make-up, checked my reflection in the mirror, and then took a deep breath before leaving the room. A maid was already making the rounds, changing linens in one of the guest rooms, and downstairs came the bright sound of cutlery hitting the porcelain of a plate. It seemed like I wasn't the only one up this early on New Year's day.

"Up already?" My father asked me, one eyebrow cocked as he saw me come down the stairs. He sat by the large dining table all by himself, a plate with fried bacon and scrambled eggs in front of him. "How are you feeling?"

"I'm fine."

"Fine, huh?" He echoed, a smirk on his lips. "Are you going to tell me you don't have a hangover?"

"Dad, I already told you," I sighed. "I had a couple of

drinks last night. I mean, it was New Year's Eve. What's the harm in it?"

"There's no harm in a little celebrating, Sibyl. Thing is, I think you're overdoing it. You're out partying and drinking almost every day of the week. Don't you think enough's enough?"

"Come on, Dad." Sitting on one of the chairs beside him, I gave the butler a little smile as he quickly placed a plate similar to my father's in front of me. "I think that's my cue. Don't you think last night was enough? Or are you going to lose it again?"

"Last night?" He asked me, furrowing his brow. "What are you talking about, Sibyl?"

"You shouted at me."

"I shouted at you?"

"That's what I said." If I sounded annoyed, that's because I was. Sure, I got home completely drunk, but it seemed like my father had had a few drinks himself. How could he not remember the way he had shouted at me? "Were you drunk last night or something? That would be ironic."

"I didn't have anything to drink," he insisted. "Seriously, I have no idea what you're talking about."

"Whatever." Rolling my eyes, I finished off the food on my plate and pushed my chair back. I was about to march out of the house when I suddenly felt guilty about the way I was acting. I turned on my heels and walked toward my father. Leaning into him, I kissed his cheek. "I love you, Dad."

"And I love you, Sibyl," he replied, sounding more tired than I ever remembered him to be. He looked up at me, managed a weak smile, and then returned his attention to his breakfast. Not knowing what else to do, I headed out of the house and hopped inside the car.

"Take me to Hops," I told the AI, and soon enough the Mayor's mansion was nothing but a small dot in the scenery. A few miles ahead of the car, the tall buildings that occupied most of Kaster's city centre rose like snow capped mountains. It would have been a beautiful New Year's day, but it was hard to feel excited about...well, about anything.

I thought of my father, alone in a house big enough for God knows how many families, and I thought of my mother. Life had been so much easier when the three of us were a family. After she passed away, it had been like a permanent fog had settled over my life.

"*We've arrived at the destination*," the AI droned half an hour later as it settled into a vacant spot on the skyport. The door slid open effortlessly, and I stepped outside, the warmth of the mall immediately making me regret my decision to bring a sweater. The girls were already there, standing in front of Hop's, the coffee shop where we usually gathered to gossip and cure our hangovers.

"How are you doing? Brain still foggy?" Aman laughed, and I just gave her a shrug. She had bags under her eyes, and her make up was all wrong. Her hair was slightly dishevelled as well, and she sounded as if she was exhausted.

"At least I got some sleep," I laughed with her. "You haven't gone to bed, have you?"

"Is it that obvious?" She grimaced, and the other three girls just rolled their eyes. Even though they weren't what I'd call close friends, this small group had been a constant in my life ever since my mother's passing. Whenever there was a party, they were always there, and they made sure to drag me along for the ride.

Together, we stepped inside the two-story coffee house and settled down on a large table by the corner, one that gave us a panoramic view of the city below. We used the touchscreen on the table to make our order, and soon enough a waiter appeared with five coffees on a tray, our names scribbled on the cups.

"Have I told you that Sibyl ditched an entire group of guys last night?" Aman said in a conspiratorial tone, and the other girls just raised their eyebrows at me. "I'm dead serious. They were buying her shots, crazy with the way she was dancing, and she just blew them off. They were cute too."

"Oh my God," Lisandre said, her accent making it

obvious to within earshot that she had been born and bred in Nyheim. "What's up with you, Sibyl? You're such a tease. You gotta move past the flirting."

"The fun is in the flirting," I said with a laugh. I had always been a nice quiet girl and, even though I had grown accustomed to all the partying, I wasn't as crazy about men as the four of them were. Sure, I enjoyed all the dancing and flirting, but that was it. None of the men I came across in the nightclubs or bars seemed to hold my interest for more than a couple of minutes. I wasn't exactly a prude, but I had my limits.

Maybe I was just picky.

Thankfully, the conversation drifted away from me after a few more laughs. Aman was recounting how she had met a guy in the last club she had gone to, and she had spent the night at his place. After a wild night of drinking and dancing between the sheets, she had rolled out of bed just so she could meet us for coffee.

As the girls talked and laughed, I stared out the window and watched the snowflakes slowly drift past me. I thought back to my conversation with my father and sighed. I knew I couldn't go on like this forever, partying every single night and trying to ignore the fact that I was now an adult, but I didn't really know how to change things.

The drinking, the dancing, and the partying...those things kept me distracted from all the things I didn't want to face. I had lost my mother, my relationship with my father had seen better days, and I had absolutely no sense of purpose. It was hard to feel motivated about anything with all those things weighing me down.

I wanted to be a better woman, no doubt about it.

I just didn't know how to go about it.

"Oh my God," Lisandre snorted, discreetly pointing to somewhere behind me. "Can you believe that?"

I turned on my chair to see a small girl of five pestering a tall Valorni. He was hunched over a table in the corner, quietly drinking from a tall cup of coffee, and the young girl seemed fascinated by the alien's size. She was peppering him with a thousand questions and, even though he was enormous in size, he was patiently answering her, a wide smile on his lips. The kid's parents watched a table to the side, amused with the situation.

"What about it?" I asked Lisandre, and she just cocked one eyebrow up.

"Are you serious right now? Like, her parents are completely irresponsible, don't you think? They're letting a kid talk to one of those monsters. Like, if I had a kid, I would never let her alone with one of them, that much I can tell you."

The other girls nodded their agreement, and I just looked at them not knowing what to say. "Please, don't tell me you're into that anti-alien stuff as well," I finally breathed out. "Don't you have anything more important to think about?"

"This is important," Lisandre insisted. "My father tells me these things are taking our jobs, and God knows what else they might be planning to do. I mean, they handle a lot of security in the city. Doesn't it make you feel like you're a prisoner?"

"That's so stupid," I snapped. "Do you really think these guys want to hurt us? Just take a look at them. If they wanted to, they could've taken over all our cities already. And have you forgotten they were the ones stopping Kaster from turning into a pile of rubble during the war?" I shook my head then, more to myself than to them, and found myself going up to my feet. "You know what? I think I'm going home."

They called my name as I walked out of the coffee shop, but I just ignored them. My headache was slowly returning, and I was in no mood to discuss the sociological implications of having aliens in our cities. If I wanted to be bored out of my mind, I could've stayed home with my father. Besides, why the hell were people so obsessed with the damn aliens? Sure, they looked scary as hell, but all they seemed to want was a regular life. That was a curious thought: these aliens wanted the exact same thing I did.

Maybe I had more in common with them than with my group of my friends.

Get Cazak Now!

https://elinwynbooks.com/conquered-world-alien-romance/

Given: Star Breed Book One

When a renegade thief and a genetically enhanced mercenary collide, space gets a whole lot hotter!

Thief Kara Shimsi has learned three lessons well - keep her head down, her fingers light, and her tithes to the syndicate paid on time.

But now a failed heist has earned her a death sentence - a one-way ticket to the toxic Waste outside the dome. Her only chance is a deal with the syndicate's most ruthless enforcer, a wolfish mountain of genetically-modified muscle named Davien.

The thought makes her body tingle with dread-or is it heat?

Mercenary Davien has one focus: do whatever is necessary to get the credits to get off this backwater mining colony and back into space. The last thing he wants is a smart-mouthed thief - even if she does have the clue he needs to hunt down whoever attacked the floating lab he and his created brothers called home.

Caring is a liability. Desire is a commodity. And love could get you killed.

https://elinwynbooks.com/star-breed/

ABOUT THE AUTHOR

I love old movies – *To Catch a Thief*, *Notorious*, *All About Eve* — and anything with Katherine Hepburn in it. Clever, elegant people doing clever, elegant things.

I'm a hopeless romantic.

And I love science fiction and the promise of space.

So it makes perfect sense to me to try to merge all of those loves into a new science fiction world, where dashing heroes and lovely ladies have adventures, get into trouble, and find their true love in the stars!

www.ingramcontent.com/pod-product-compliance
Lightning Source LLC
Chambersburg PA
CBHW070736180626
46818CB00007B/2873